Fair Has Nothing to Do With It

Fair Has Nothing to Do With It

Cynthia Cotten

Farrar, Straus and Giroux ✎ New York

Distributed in Canada by Douglas & McIntyre Ltd.
Printed in the United States of America
Designed by Jay Colvin
First edition, 2007
1 3 5 7 9 10 8 6 4 2

www.fsgkidsbooks.com

Library of Congress Cataloging-in-Publication Data
Cotten, Cynthia.
Fair has nothing to do with it / Cynthia Cotten.— 1st ed.
p. cm.
Summary: When Michael's beloved grandfather dies, he has a hard time admitting how much it hurts and allowing himself to trust anyone again.
ISBN-13: 978-0-374-39935-1
ISBN-10: 0-374-39935-2
[1. Grief—Fiction. 2. Grandfathers—Fiction. 3. Drawing—Fiction.] I. Title.

PZ7.C82865 Fai 2007
[Fic]—dc22

2006045170

Dedicated to the memories of two men:
my father, William W. Storrs, teacher and
painter, whose life touched so many others, and
my father-in-law, Floyd Cotten, Jr.,
a quiet man who loved the land

Fair Has Nothing to Do With It

One

"Grandpa said I could drive the tractor myself this year." Michael shifted in his seat so he could face Mom.

"What?" Mom glanced away from the road, a look of concern in her eyes. "Oh, Michael, I don't know about that."

"He said you'd probably say that."

"He did, did he?"

"Yeah. And he said you were driving it when you were twelve."

"That's different. I grew up around those machines."

"So?"

"So, a couple of weeks in the summer isn't enough time to get familiar with that tractor. It's old, and it can be tricky."

"Come on, Mom, I'm almost thirteen. I've been driving with him for the last couple of years. I'll be careful."

"Okay—you've made your point. I'll talk it over with Grandpa. But I'm not making any promises."

Her voice had that tone—the one Michael knew

meant it was best to let the subject drop for now. "I wish Dad could have come," he said.

"So do I," Mom said. "But he wants to get his dissertation written. It's the last step in finishing his Ph.D."

Michael groaned. "I know. But why does he want to teach college math? Doesn't he like teaching high school math anymore?"

"Michael, we've been over this a dozen times. It's something he's always wanted to do. And he's looking ahead. You'll be ready for college sooner than you think, then so will your sisters. A college teaching job often means free tuition."

"I know. But, Mom, we hardly see him at all anymore. During the school year he was at work all day, and down at the university at night. I thought that once summer came he'd be around more, but he's not. And even when he is home, he's in his office. It's not fair."

Mom sighed. "Michael, please, give it a rest. Do you think it's easy on him?"

"I don't know."

"Think about it," Mom continued. "He has his job during the school year. He's been researching and writing his dissertation. And it's a forty-five-minute drive one way between home and the university."

"So?"

"So, do you see him dancing for joy at having to spend his summer this way? We knew before he began this graduate work that it would be hard on all of us. Right?"

Michael stared at his shoes. "Right."

"It won't be like this forever. Really." She smiled. "For the next couple of weeks, you and I and the girls will just have to try and have a good time at the farm without him."

Michael glanced over his shoulder to the backseat, where his two sisters were still napping. "I guess so," he said. It would be tough, though. Dad loved Grandma and Grandpa Currie's farm, even though he was more a computer geek than a country boy. He said it was the one place where he could always relax. Sometimes they had a family picnic at a lake near the farm and he and Dad had stone-skipping contests. Or they played basketball, using the old hoop that had been on the front of the garage ever since Mom and Uncle Paul had been kids. And sometimes they just sat out on the lawn, Dad with a book and Michael with a sketch pad, enjoying some lazy time together. But now Dad was too busy to have fun or be lazy. He was too busy for anything but work.

Rustling noises came from the backseat, then "Will we be there soon?" came Jamie's voice.

"Not much longer now," Mom said. "We're off the Interstate, so maybe another half hour."

"Mama, can we pick berries at Grandma's?" Molly asked.

"I don't know if there'll be any ripe ones, sweetie," Mom said. "Early August might be a little early. But if there are any ready, Grandma will be counting on you to pick them."

"Michael, too?"

"I can't," Michael said. "I'll be doing real work with Grandpa."

Mom kept her eyes on the road. "We'll see," is all she said.

Michael settled back in his seat and looked out the window. He liked this part of the trip the best. The road wound along past rolling meadows dotted with black-and-white cows, and fields of corn, wheat, and hay, all different shades of green. By the end of the month the wheat would be turning gold, just like in the van Gogh painting in Mom's college art history book, the one she gave him last year.

"Molly, play fair!"

He sighed. Four hours was a long time to be buckled into the car, especially for live wires like Jamie and Molly, so they made up games. Usually the one they called Counting Cows kept them quiet and happy for a while. Not today, though.

"I saw them first."

"No, you didn't. They were on my side!"

"That doesn't matter, Molly. You didn't say anything, so I get them."

"They're *my* cows!"

"Look, girls, there's the water tower. We're almost there." Mom's voice was cheery, but she gripped the steering wheel as if she were trying to choke it.

"Ow!"

"Mama!"

Mom took a deep breath and bit her lower lip. She

pulled the car onto the shoulder of the road and shut off the engine. "That's enough!" She turned around and glared at the girls. "I can't concentrate on driving with the two of you fighting. For heaven's sake, Jamie, anyone listening to you would wonder if you're really eight years old. You sound more like another four-year-old."

She faced forward and started the car again. Michael glanced at the girls. Molly was acting as if nothing had happened, and Jamie wore her best thundercloud face. When she saw Michael looking at her, she kicked the back of his seat, hard.

Up ahead, an old white barn that belonged to one of Grandpa's neighbors listed toward the road. "It's still there," Michael said. "I wonder how much farther it can lean before it falls right over."

"I don't know," Mom said. "It's been there as long as I can remember. You know what Grandpa says, though." She lowered her voice and raised one eyebrow. "Nothing lasts forever, Mickey. When its time comes—"

Michael joined in. "—it'll go."

They both laughed. "I swear," Mom said, shaking her head, "he used to make me crazy when I was growing up. It seemed as if he had a saying or a comment for everything. But, you know, the older I got, the more sense he made."

She turned the car off the main road just beyond the white barn. Michael and the girls broke into a cheer. "We're almost there!" Jamie shouted. "There's the horse barn."

"Yay!" Molly clapped her hands.

"Why is it called the horse barn?" Jamie asked. "Grandpa doesn't have any horses."

"He did when I was growing up," Mom said. "Now he keeps equipment in it. But everyone called it the horse barn for so long that the name just stuck."

"I see the creek," Michael said, "and a heron. Look—he's got a fish."

He and Grandpa would go fishing tomorrow, at the pond on the far north end of the farm. They always did his first day there. It was their special time. Sometimes they talked about school, or the farm, or growing up. Other times they just sat quietly, listening to the cicadas buzz and the carp slurp. Whatever they did, though, it was always just Michael and Grandpa.

"There's the hay barn," Jamie said, "and the house."

Michael straightened in his seat. "Hey, Mom, what's going on up there?"

Several vehicles were parked by the white farmhouse, and an ambulance was just pulling out of the driveway. It drove away in the other direction.

"Oh, no." Mom slowed the car to a stop, right in the middle of the road. She looked scared.

"Their lights weren't flashing," Michael said, "and they weren't using the siren. They were probably just collecting for the ambulance fund, like they do every summer."

She gave him a quick, tight little smile. "You're right," she said, and stepped on the gas. A moment later, she pulled into the driveway and parked the car where she always did, on the grass under the old crab apple tree.

As they all piled out of the car, Grandma came across the lawn toward them, wiping her eyes with a dish towel. As she got closer, it looked as if she'd been crying a lot.

"You three wait here," Mom said. She ran and put her arms around Grandma. Michael heard her say, "Oh, Mom, when?" They talked softly for a moment, then Grandma started back to the house. Mom called after her, "We'll be right there."

She turned to Michael and the girls, wiping her own eyes. Michael knew before a word was said that things weren't going to be anything like he had planned. Looking Mom straight in the eye, he asked, "What's wrong with Grandpa?"

TWO

They sat on the ground near the car. Nobody said a word.

Michael plucked at the grass, carefully tearing the slim green blades in two and letting them fall. He concentrated on the growing pile of green shreds, trying to sort out the jumble of thoughts bouncing around in his head. Grandpa—dead? He couldn't be. That ambulance was taking him away. But they were supposed to go fishing tomorrow. He couldn't be dead. What about Grandma?

Molly's voice broke the silence. "Was Grandpa sick, Mama?"

Mom sniffled and wiped her eyes with the edge of her shirt. "Not exactly," she said. "But his heart wasn't as strong as it used to be, before the attack he had a few years ago. You remember that, don't you, Michael?"

Michael thought back. "Yeah. You came to stay with Grandma for a while." He tore at another blade of grass. "But Grandpa got better. He did what the doctor told him, and he was okay."

The summer after Grandpa's heart attack was when the two of them started going for long walks after dinner. "Time for our constitutional, Mickey," Grandpa would call, and off they'd go. They always found something interesting—a killdeer's nest, fresh deer tracks, a hawk feather. Once in a while they even found an arrowhead, left by a hunter who had been there a long time ago.

Jamie interrupted his thoughts. "But, Mama, if Grandpa did what the doctor told him, why did he die?"

Mom didn't say anything for a moment. "I don't know, Jamie," she said at last. "Grandpa lived a long time, and he worked hard. Maybe his heart was just worn out."

"But, Mama—" Molly began.

"Molly, cut it out!" Michael snapped.

"All right," Mom said, "that's enough. Take it easy, Michael. We're all upset." She looked toward the house and took a deep, shaky breath. "We'd better go in," she said. "Come on, everybody, grab your stuff."

Michael, Jamie, and Molly followed Mom to the kitchen door inside the garage. Coming down the two wooden steps from the door was a tall man with a tan, lined face. Mom's brother, Uncle Paul. His usually smiling eyes were red-rimmed. "I'm glad you're here, Ellie," he said to Mom.

Mom hugged him. "How did it happen?" she asked.

"All I know is that he was across the road, on the tractor, spraying the potatoes," Uncle Paul said. "Mom saw him stop and get off. She figured one of the sprays had gotten plugged and he was fixing it. But after a while, when he didn't get back on again, she got worried and went to check. She found him lying on the ground."

A shiver washed over Michael. He closed his eyes, fighting the picture in his mind.

Uncle Paul said goodbye, and they went up the steps and into the kitchen. Grandma was on the phone. "Now listen, you three," Mom said in a low voice. "I have to try and get hold of Dad when she's finished, and then she and Uncle Paul and I have to talk about arrangements. So, Michael, I'm putting you in charge of keeping your sisters occupied and quiet. Molly and Jamie, listen to your brother and don't bother Grandma. Okay?"

They nodded.

When Grandma hung up the phone, she came over and hugged them all without saying a word.

Mom put an arm around Grandma's shoulders, saying, "Why don't you rest out here while I make some phone calls." She led her through the dining room, out to the screened porch.

Molly took a step to follow them, but Michael caught her arm. "Leave her alone," he said. Taking Jamie's shoulder with his other hand, he steered them into the living room. "In here," he said. "You heard Mom. Find something to do. And keep it quiet."

While the girls argued about what game to play, Michael listened to Mom on the phone. Where was Dad, anyway? He wasn't at home, so Mom left a message on the machine for him to call her. Then she called the university and left messages with his adviser and at both the computer center and the library.

By late afternoon, Dad still hadn't called. Jamie and Molly were growing more and more cranky, and Michael had just about had it. How was Dad supposed to get through if the line was always busy, he wondered as he heard Mom field another call about Grandpa. "Want me to read to you?" he asked Molly, grabbing her hand before she could throw a handful of dominoes at Jamie.

"No," she said. "When's Grandpa coming home?"

Didn't she understand? "Molly," Michael said, "he's not coming home."

"Ever?"

He shook his head.

Jamie sniffled. Then she broke into a loud wail. Molly, who usually did whatever Jamie did, joined in.

Now what? He was supposed to be keeping them quiet, and instead they were howling like a couple of animals.

In a matter of seconds, Mom was there. She took the girls into her arms. "It's okay," she said to Michael over Molly's blond head. "I'll take it from here."

Relieved, Michael headed for the living room. Grandma was coming down the stairs. She smiled at him, and her eyes began to water. "Just yesterday, he was out there making sure his fishing gear was ready," she said. "He was so looking forward . . . like a little boy . . ." Tears ran down her face.

Michael swallowed, hard. What was he supposed to

do? He reached out and hugged Grandma, patting her shoulder.

Almost as quickly as her tears had begun, they stopped. She stepped back and wiped her eyes with the back of her hand.

Michael opened his mouth, but nothing came out. It was as if everything inside him had frozen up. The words to tell Grandma how much he was going to miss Grandpa just wouldn't come.

After a moment, Grandma said, "That's all right, Michael." She went into the kitchen, and Michael headed up the stairs to his room. He closed the door, went over to the window, and leaned his head against the glass.

A few minutes later, there was a knock on the door. The hinges squeaked, then Mom said, "How are you doing?"

"Okay, I guess," he said, turning around.

"Dad just called. He'll be here around ten-thirty."

"Okay."

"I'm going to fix some sandwiches. What would you like?"

"I don't think I want anything."

She frowned. "Are you sure? We ate lunch around eleven—have you had anything since then?"

"The girls and I each had a couple of cookies a while ago."

"You should eat something, then."

"Mom, I'm not hungry. Really."

She sighed. "All right. Maybe later." She closed the

door and went back downstairs, the wooden steps creaking beneath her feet.

Michael sat down on the old, saggy bed that had been Mom's when she was his age. He fidgeted with a frayed spot on the blanket binding. Then he dug into his dark green duffel bag and pulled out his sketch pad. He flipped back page after page until he came to a blank one. Fishing a pencil out of the bag, he began to draw just random lines, focusing all his attention on the rhythmic movement of his hand. Gradually, the lines began to form a shape—a barn that listed to one side. He stopped and studied what he'd drawn, then ripped the page off the pad, crumpled it, and threw it across the room. He did this two or three times more, then tossed the pad and pencil onto the bed.

He needed some air.

Even though he knew everyone was out on the porch, he went down the stairs as quietly as he could. As he reached the bottom, the phone began to ring. He thought about answering it, then stopped. It was sure to be another call about Grandpa. Letting it ring, he slipped out the kitchen door, through the garage, and up into the fields behind the house, fields where he and Grandpa had walked so often.

He walked and walked, until his legs ached. When he came back to the house, the sun was getting low, glowing soft red over the woods to the west.

He sat down on the swing that hung from a limb of the old maple tree in the front yard. He hadn't used this swing since he was Jamie's age. He closed his eyes, letting the swaying motion rock him while the rustling leaves whispered overhead.

He scuffed the grass with his right toe. Mom's explanation wasn't good enough. There had to be more. Did the doctor forget to tell Grandpa something? Or did he tell him something wrong?

A little hunger pang poked at his stomach. Better eat something now. He went inside. On the kitchen table was a plate with a sandwich. He lifted the top slice of bread. Peanut butter with raspberry jam—his favorite. Mom must have left it for him.

She was upstairs with the girls, probably getting them ready for bed. He peeked into the living room. Grandma was in her favorite chair. Her head leaned against the back of the chair, and little snores escaped her open mouth.

He picked up the sandwich and went back outside, around to the front yard. Between the maple tree and the house were two aluminum lawn chairs where he and Grandpa used to sit and watch the night fall. He sat down on one of them and bit into the sandwich.

The rosy afterglow of the sunset was fading fast. Up the road, the horse barn loomed like a great shadow against the darkening sky. Heat lightning flashed in the distance, and fireflies twinkled around the yard.

It was the time of evening when aromas hung heavy in the air. A light breeze brought the faint sweetness of corn and potato plants, and a musty smell from the hay barn across from the house.

As Michael sat, he could hear cars on the main road,

crickets chirping in the lawn, and a dog barking somewhere on the other side of the woods. Up in a tree a bird called, once, twice, and then was silent.

Anyone who thinks the country is a quiet place has never really paid attention, Mickey.

How many times had he heard Grandpa say that? He'd always thought Grandpa was kidding. After all, compared to the town Michael lived in, the country was quiet. But tonight he realized for the first time what Grandpa had meant. There were so many sounds and sights and smells that he loved and looked forward to every summer, things that always made him feel so alive. Now, though, he wished he could block it all out. He didn't want to feel anything.

He jumped up and walked around the side of the house and across the yard to the little shed that was Grandpa's workshop.

He opened the door and flipped on the wall switch, blinking at the sudden light. As he stepped inside and closed the door, he saw Grandpa's fishing rod, tackle box, and landing net lying on the workbench. He walked over and gently opened the tackle box. "Oh, Grandpa," he whispered, his voice breaking.

How could he drop out of Michael's life without a word of warning? It wasn't fair.

Michael picked up the net and turned it over in his hands. He smiled as he remembered the first time Grandpa had let him use it. That fish had been only about four inches long, but Grandpa had been so excited it might as well have measured closer to a foot. A lump formed in his throat, and as he swallowed it down, his smile went with it. "Why?" he cried, hurling the net across the little room. It hit an empty shelf and fell to the floor.

As quickly as it had flared, his anger subsided, leaving him cold and numb inside. He picked up the net and ran his fingers along the dull metal handle, wincing at a dent that hadn't been there before, then put it back on the workbench.

A screen door and a car door banged shut at the same time. Michael looked at his watch. Nine forty-five. If that was Dad, he'd cut a four-hour drive down to a little more than three.

He turned off the light, stepped out of the shed, and started running across the yard. At the corner of the house, he stopped.

In the blue glow of the yard light, he saw Dad in the driveway with Mom in his arms. Her shoulders shook, and from where he stood Michael could hear her sobs.

Michael cleared his throat. Mom and Dad looked over at him, and each held out an arm. As he ran to them, throwing himself into their hug, tears spilled from his eyes. He pressed his face against Dad's shoulder and let them flow.

At last, he pulled back and drew in a long, shaky breath that finished with a hiccup. Dad squeezed his shoulder. When Mom spoke, her voice trembled. "I was starting to worry about you."

Michael looked at his shoes. "Sorry."

"Where have you been?"

"Just walking. I've been back for a while. I was in the workshop." He paused. "Thanks for the sandwich."

She smiled, just a little. "You're welcome. Why don't you go on in now. We'll be right along."

"Okay." Michael rubbed his eyes and headed around the house to the kitchen door. He suddenly felt very tired.

A few minutes later, he climbed into bed and turned off the light. Dad was here. Maybe things would be better tomorrow.

Three

The sun on his face woke Michael the next morning. He looked at the clock and groaned. Seven o'clock. Why couldn't Grandma have window shades instead of those curtains you could see right through? He rolled over and closed his eyes again, but it was no use. He was awake.

The house was still as he threw on his clothes, swiped at his face with a damp washcloth, and tiptoed down the stairs. He poured cereal into a bowl and splashed some milk on it. Picking up a spoon, he held it over the bowl, listening to the quiet snapping as the milk soaked into the tiny puffs.

A sudden burst of melody drew him to the window. A small brown wren sat at one of the feeders Grandma kept filled all year. The bird cocked its head at him, warbled again, and flew away.

He heard footsteps upstairs. Whoever it was would be down shortly. He gulped a few bites of cereal. Then, putting his bowl in the sink, he opened the kitchen door as quietly as he could and headed outside.

The sun was already burning off the early morning haze as he walked down the driveway, across the road, and along one of the rough dirt lanes that crisscrossed the green fields. He stopped to look at the alfalfa on his left. The air hummed like electric lines as honeybees darted here and there among the deep blue blossoms. It looked good, just about ready to cut. Who would take care of that now?

Skree—ee—eech! He snapped his head up just in time to see a hawk dive into the bean field near the woods, then rise back into the air with something in its talons. Something that had been alive just seconds before.

A voice behind him called, "Hold up there, Michael!"

It was Dad, half walking, half jogging to catch up. "You don't make it easy for a guy," he panted as he stopped next to Michael.

"Out of shape?" Michael gave him an elbow nudge. "Maybe you need to take some time off."

"Maybe we'd better talk about something else," Dad said.

"Okay." Michael started walking again.

Dad fell into step with him. "It's going to be another hot one today."

"Uh-huh."

Neither of them said anything more for a few minutes. Then, "Hawk!" Dad said, pointing upward.

Michael glanced at the sky. "That's a turkey buzzard."

"Are you sure?"

"Yeah. It's darker than a hawk. See how its wings splay out and tip up, and how it tilts from side to side as it flies? Look—there are a couple more."

"All right, all right." Dad smiled. "You've convinced me."

At the top of a little rise, Michael grabbed Dad's arm. "Deer," he whispered. "Three of them, at the far edge of the beans."

Dad looked off to the right.

"No, Dad, the beans are over there," Michael said.

Dad turned his head. "Shouldn't we scare them off?" he murmured.

Michael tightened his grip. "Not today." He held Dad's arm a moment longer, then let go. "Grandpa said once that planting so close to the woods was like giving the deer an engraved invitation. But he did it anyway."

The deer ate a few minutes longer. Suddenly one of them picked up its head and looked straight at Dad and Michael, then all three deer bounded back into the woods. When they were gone, Dad smiled at Michael. "Grandpa taught you a lot about nature, didn't he?"

Michael nodded.

"I never had that," Dad continued. "I was a city kid. In fact, when your mother and I were first dating, she used to joke that I didn't know the difference between a rooster and a goat. You're lucky you had such a good teacher."

Michael nodded again, heat growing behind his eyes. *Stop it, Dad, please.*

"You know," Dad said, "maybe you could teach me—"

"Dad, don't."

Dad stood silent for a moment. "I guess I'll go back to the house," he said at last. "Mom and the girls are probably up by now."

"Fine."

"Calling hours at the funeral home begin at two, so we'll be leaving around one-thirty."

"I know."

"I brought your good clothes with me."

"Thanks."

"Michael."

Michael looked up, then away from the hurt in Dad's eyes.

"I know this is rough, and I can see you don't feel like talking right now," Dad said. "But if you do, I'm here, okay?"

"Okay." *For how long?*

He watched Dad start down the lane toward the house before continuing on alone.

He hated the idea of going to the funeral home. At least the calling times were just this afternoon and this evening, and he and the girls only had to go this afternoon. Grandpa had said after his first heart attack, "I want two things when I do go: only one day of visiting, and a closed casket. Then get me in the ground. No use in prolonging the sadness." Grandma had tried to talk him out of it. "That's awfully fast," she said. "And what about the people who'd want to come but couldn't make it on such short notice?" "That won't be my problem," Grandpa had said with a chuckle. Grandma had finally given in, saying if that was the way he wanted it, that's how it would be.

On the way to the funeral home, Michael sat in the backseat, jammed between Jamie and Molly. Dad had been right about one thing—the day had turned into a real scorcher. Sweat was already dripping down his back, and if he loosened his tie any more he'd never tighten it again. At least he didn't have to put on his jacket until the last minute.

When they got there, Michael stared at the sign out in front. Graves' Funeral Home? Graves? Some kind of joke, right? But no, Grandma was introducing them all to Mr. Graves, who took them into a cool, wood-paneled room where the smell of flowers was almost overpowering.

Grandpa's casket was at the front of the room. Jamie said to Molly, "Let's go look." Michael hung back, watching as they walked up and smelled the flowers and ran their fingers over the smoothness of the polished wooden lid. They seemed so comfortable. Didn't they know Grandpa was in there?

Grandma went and stood with them, stroking their hair and speaking softly. He hoped she would be all right this afternoon. She'd been crying all morning. Mom had tried to get her to take one of the pills the doctor had left yesterday, but she had refused. "I don't want my friends to see me all doped up," she'd said firmly. She seemed calm right now. But Michael could see her clenching and unclenching a tissue in her left hand.

Once again, Mom had put him in charge of the girls, who had each brought a coloring book and a plastic bag full of crayons. He got them settled at one end of a couch at the back of the room and sat down at the other end.

People were starting to come in now. He watched as they hugged Grandma and Mom, and shook hands with Dad and Uncle Paul and his family. Some of the women wiped their eyes, and the men all looked very serious. Grandma was fine until her best friend, Vera, came in and hugged her. Then she broke down and sobbed and had to be helped to a small room off to the side. When she came out a short time later, she went to a chair and sat down, her eyes red and puffy and her hands trembling.

After a while, none of it seemed real. It was as if he were watching everything on a big screen. He let his eyes pan the room like a movie camera.

People, people, flowers, casket. The sight of the casket jerked him back. This was no movie. He stood up and walked around, busying himself with things like reading the guest book, counting bald heads, and trying to imagine what some of these old people would have looked like at his age. Anything to keep his mind off why he was there.

It only lasted a couple of hours, but to Michael it seemed like forever. When they got home he raced upstairs and put on shorts and a T-shirt, leaving his good clothes in a heap on his bed. As he went into the hall he heard his parents' voices through the door of their room. Mom sounded upset. "Why can't you stay on for a few extra days?" she was saying.

"Ellen, I told you last night," Dad said. "Kirk's my adviser. He's going to be leaving town for three weeks, and I have to see him before he goes."

"So call him."

"It wouldn't do any good. All my papers are at home."

"But, Jim—"

"Ellen, listen—I wanted to get the whole first draft written by the end of the summer, before I have to start teaching again in September. Well, that's not going to happen. But there's just one section left to write, and Kirk wants to talk with me before I start. I have to do this, honey."

"Jim, I know this graduate work is important." Mom's voice was quiet, careful, as if she were trying to choose just the right words. "We all do. But under the circumstances—"

"Ellen, I'm sorry. I wish I could stay. But I have to go back in a couple of days."

"Fine." A drawer slammed.

"Ellen," Dad said in a pleading voice.

Silence.

Michael heard footsteps come toward the door, and ducked back into his room. He heard Dad stomp down the stairs and go out the kitchen door. Then he stuck his head into the hall and listened. Mom was crying.

He went downstairs and found Jamie and Molly in the kitchen. "Grandma's asleep on the porch," Jamie said. "Daddy went outside."

"He's mad," Molly said. "Can we have something to eat?"

"Sure. Peanut butter crackers?"

"Okay. With lots of peanut butter."

Michael fixed Molly's crackers, and some for himself, and let Jamie do her own. As he put Molly's plate on the table, she said, "Is Grandpa really in that box?"

"What?" Michael said.

"Is Grandpa really in that box?" Molly repeated.

"Yes," Michael said. "Now eat."

"Why is he?"

"Because he's dead, dummy," Jamie said.

"Can we open it and look at him sometimes?" Molly asked.

Jamie, still at the counter, started to snicker.

"Jamie, don't," Michael warned.

She ignored him. "Open it?" she said. "Don't you know what they're going to do with that box?"

Molly shook her head.

"Jamie, cut it out!" Michael said.

"They're going to bury it," Jamie said. "And pretty soon he's going to start falling apart."

Molly stared at her sister, openmouthed. Then she fled from the kitchen, crying, "Mama! Mama!"

Michael reached over, grabbed Jamie's shoulder, and gave it a little shake. "That was great," he said. "Mom really needs this right now."

Jamie shrugged away from his grip and put the lid on the peanut butter jar. "I just told the truth," she said.

"You make me want to puke." Michael went out the door, into the garage.

He sat on the step just outside the kitchen door, watching a couple of hornets buzz around a window. There was so much stuff in here—Grandma's freezer, Grandpa's lawn tractor, the woodpile, and lots more—that there was never enough room for any kind of vehicle. Everyone always parked outside in the driveway, or on the grass.

The woodpile was huge. Grandpa cut the wood in the summer so it would have time to dry, and there was enough to keep the stove in the living room and the fireplace in the TV den going all winter. The chunks were pretty big, though. Grandma was going to need someone to split them for her.

He could hear Mom in the kitchen, yelling at Jamie. By sliding back and putting his ear against the door, he managed to catch bits and pieces of what she said as they filtered through—"at your age," "use your head," and "what were you thinking of?" Jamie gave her an answer he couldn't make out.

"Anything interesting?" The voice behind him made him jump. He looked up and saw Dad standing there, arms folded across his chest. In one hand was a big bunch of wildflowers—soft blue chicory, bright yellow buttercups, and pale Queen Anne's lace.

Michael felt his face grow hot. "Uh, well, not really, I guess."

"You'd better be careful. You might hear things you'll wish you hadn't."

Tell me about it.

"Do you know where Mom is?"

"In the kitchen." Michael moved over so Dad could open the door.

Maybe he's changed his mind, he thought after Dad had gone inside. *Maybe he's going to stay longer. Please, please let that be it.* He didn't know how long he sat there, repeating those words over and over. But after a while the door opened and Mom said, "Oh, good, you're right here. Would you come in, please?"

Michael walked into the kitchen on heavy legs. Dad, Jamie, and Molly were already there. He pulled out the chair farthest from Dad and sat down.

"We need to talk about tomorrow," Mom said.

"What's tomorrow?" Jamie asked.

"Grandpa's funeral," Mom said. "Eleven o'clock tomorrow morning. The service will be at the funeral home, then we'll all go to the cemetery."

"I don't want to go," Michael said, saying aloud what he'd been thinking since they'd come back from the funeral home. He kept his eyes on the table, waiting for them to start in on him.

"Why, Michael?" Mom said. Her voice wasn't angry or surprised. Just quiet.

He couldn't find the words. "I just don't want to."

She reached over and covered his hand with hers. "There won't be another chance, you know."

He nodded, not daring to look at her.

"Now, wait a minute," Dad said. "Michael, I think you should be there."

"I don't want to go," Michael said. "And if you make me go, I won't stay."

Dad opened his mouth, but Mom said quickly, "It's all right, Jim." She looked hard at Michael. "Are you absolutely sure about this?" He nodded. "Fine, Michael. We'll respect your decision. I'll talk to Grandma."

"Thanks. Can I go now?"

She let go of his hand and he went back out to the garage. He leaned against the kitchen door, drained and shaking, the unspoken arguments ringing in his head. *Scared? What about Grandma? They'll all wonder where you are. You won't get another chance. Chance for what? To say goodbye.* "Stop it!" he said, shaking his head. When his mind was quiet again, he stood up straight. "I'm sorry, Grandpa," he whispered. "I just can't do it."

The next morning, Michael sat on his bed drawing while the rest of the family got ready for the funeral. Grandma had come in a few minutes ago, dressed all in black. She looked so different from the Grandma who usually wore brightly colored shirts and slacks or flowered dresses. When she came into the room, he'd been afraid to meet her eyes. But she came over and hugged him, saying, "I'm sure he understands, Michael."

Mom was the only one left upstairs now. She always made sure everyone else was ready first, which made Dad crazy. He hated just the thought of being late.

Michael chewed on his pencil as he looked at his drawing of an empty rowboat sitting in dark, shadowy water. Then he set the pad aside with a sigh.

"Ellen! We'd better get going!" Dad called from downstairs.

"Coming!"

The hollow sound of heels on bare wood floor came along the hallway, then there was a quiet tap on Michael's door.

"Yeah," he said.

"Hi." Mom stuck her head into the room. "We're just about ready to go." She paused. "We could wait, you know, if you wanted to—"

"I don't, Mom."

"All right. I just wanted to be sure you hadn't changed your mind."

"I haven't."

She sighed. "We'll be back in a while. And remember, people are coming here afterward."

"It's like having a party because Grandpa died," Michael grumbled.

"Not really." Mom came over to him. "It's just important for the people who loved Grandpa to be together to talk and comfort each other."

"Well, I think it's sick."

Mom shook her head. "Michael, maybe someday all this will make sense to you." A car horn honked out in the driveway. "In the meantime, please, if anyone gets here before we do, let them in and be polite. Okay?"

"Okay." He turned away from her.

"I'd better get down there," she said, kissing the top of his head. "I love you."

"You, too," he mumbled. He listened until he heard a car door close. Then he stood up, went over to the window, and watched the car go out the driveway and down the road until he couldn't see it anymore.

The silent house felt empty, as empty as he felt inside. His stomach rumbled, reminding him he hadn't eaten much breakfast. He went down to the kitchen, took a banana from a bowl on the counter, and went outside.

He had at least a couple of hours before everyone came back. Around here, he could usually come up with a dozen things to do with that much time. But not today.

He wished he had one of those cartoon holes, a black circle he could just drop somewhere and crawl into. Then, when he came back out, Grandpa'd be cutting hay and he'd be trying to block one of Dad's great dunk shots. He looked up at the basketball hoop on the garage. "Yeah, sure," he said. He lifted the lid of a trash can in the garage and dropped in the banana skin, then went back inside and up the stairs.

As he passed Grandma's room, he stopped in the open doorway. Grandpa's old blue sweater hung over the back of the rocking chair, just like always. He went in and picked it up, hugging it to his chest and breathing in the familiar Grandpa smell. As he put the sweater back, he noticed a large book on the bed. PHOTOS was on the cover in worn gold letters. Curious, he sat down and opened it.

From the first few pages, severe-looking men and women stared back at him. They wore plain, formal clothes, dark, with high collars. The brownish tones of these photos reminded him of some that he'd seen once at the historical museum. A name was written beside each one, but none of them meant anything to him.

Then he came to a picture of a man, a woman, a boy about his age, and a girl a little older. They, too, were plainly dressed, and stood stiffly on the porch of a neat white farmhouse. The woman's hand rested on the boy's shoulder as if to keep him from fidgeting. Beside the photo was written: "Hannah and James Currie, Rachel and Henry."

Henry? It was Grandpa, with his parents and Great-Aunt Rachel, and the house was this one, before the porch had been enclosed.

Funny. He'd never thought about Grandpa being a kid, but there he stood, in his Sunday best, looking uncomfortable. It looked as if he'd tried to slick his hair back, but part of it flopped forward into his eyes, just like Michael's.

More pages, more photos. Grandpa on his high school graduation day, in his army uniform, on the day he married Grandma. With each picture he grew a little older, until he began to look more like the Grandpa Michael knew. There were pictures of him with Mom and Uncle Paul as they were growing up. And then here he was with Mom, holding a baby and grinning from ear to ear. Beside the photo was written: "Our first grandchild, Michael Kevin Delaney."

Most of the photos after that were of Michael and the girls, doubles of ones Mom and Dad had taken. He skimmed through these. Then he came to one that stopped him cold: Grandpa and him, last summer, with a three-foot northern pike. Michael closed his eyes, remembering that day at the lake—how he'd hooked that fish, and the fight it had put up, swimming like a crazy fish, back and forth, first toward the boat, then away. All the time, Grandpa coached him: "Come on, Mickey, you can do this. Let him run a little. Now try to reel him back. Attaboy!" After what had seemed like hours of fighting, Michael's arms ached, but the fish still had enough strength to almost pull him right out of the boat. Grandpa caught him and steadied him, helping to hold the rod and crank the reel.

On the way home, they'd stopped at the hardware store and run into a couple of Grandpa's buddies. "That fish never had a chance," Grandpa had bragged to them. "Mickey had him right from the start." And what a racket they'd made when they pulled into the driveway, whooping out the truck windows while Grandpa blared the horn.

He opened his eyes. Was that a car door closing? He jumped to his feet and ran to the window. A car he didn't recognize stood in the driveway, and a man and woman were looking at Grandma's roses. What were they doing here already? He couldn't have spent that much time looking at the photo album. But now another car was pulling in next to the first.

Mom would kill him if he wasn't down there before she got home.

He put the album back on Grandma's bed and ran to his room. He tore off his shorts and tank top, threw on fresh chinos and a polo shirt, and ran a comb through his hair. He heard another car door close, and now someone was coming in the kitchen door. Jeez, didn't these people wait to be invited in? He raced down the stairs, wondering what he was supposed to say to them. "Be polite," Mom had said. That was a lot of help.

He didn't have to worry. Mom was already there.

"And this is our son, Michael," she said as he skidded

into the kitchen. "Michael, this is Mr. and Mrs. Lewis."

"Pleased to meet you." Michael shook hands with the couple, avoiding Mom's face and the "Where were you?" glare he knew was on it. Then Mom handed him a large covered dish, saying, "Put this in the oven, on 'warm.' " After she took the Lewises into the living room, Michael peeked into the dish. Whatever it was, it looked weird.

More and more people came. Pretty soon the living room was full, and guests spilled over into the dining room and onto the porch, laughing and talking. Were these the same people who'd been so sad at the funeral home yesterday? How could their sadness go away so fast? They couldn't have cared much about Grandpa—not the way he did.

He didn't want anything to do with any of them.

"Here." Mom was back, with another casserole dish. "Will you take charge of the food?"

"Sure." He'd be fine here in the kitchen by himself.

He was putting muffins in a basket when Jamie and Molly came in from the living room. "Can I have one?" Jamie asked.

"I don't care," he said.

"I want one, too," Molly said.

Michael handed her one and she sat down to eat it, carefully picking out all the raisins.

"Why are you doing that?" Jamie asked.

"They're the best part," Molly said. "I'm saving them for last."

Michael remembered Grandpa explaining why he always ate the frosting off a piece of cake first. "When I was little," he'd said, "I wanted to save it for last, because it was the best part. But my sister would snitch it right off my plate. Finally, I got smart and ate it first. And I guess old habits die hard."

"What are you smiling at?" Jamie asked.

"Nothing," Michael said.

Jamie narrowed her eyes. "Are too."

Mom came into the kitchen. "Okay," she said, "let's get the food on the table."

Michael handed Jamie the basket of muffins. "Put these on the table," he said before she could get started again.

Even with the extra leaf in it, the old oak table barely held everything. Michael stood in the kitchen, waiting for the guests to help themselves first. When they were done, he looked at the table. They sure hadn't taken much. If that was all they were going to eat, Grandma'd be eating leftovers for at least a month.

Dad, Grandma, and Uncle Paul and his family sat in the living room talking with people, while Mom seemed to be everywhere at once—"circulating," she called it. After a while she came into the kitchen and said to Michael, "Why don't you come in with us for a while."

"I'm okay here," Michael said.

She wasn't going to take no for an answer. "I think Grandma would like it," she said. "Besides, you're part of this family, which means they're your guests, too."

"I didn't invite them."

Mom strode to the kitchen door and opened it. "Out here," she said. "Now."

He walked past her, into the garage. She closed the door and turned to face him. "I've had just about enough, Michael. We have company here, people you like, who haven't seen you in a long time. And your attitude is downright rude."

"What about their attitude?"

"What do you mean?"

"You said they were going to talk and comfort each other, but they're all acting like they just got back from vacation. What about Grandpa?"

Mom blew out a loud breath, rubbing a hand across her face. "If you were in there," she said, "you'd know that all that talking and laughing is *about* Grandpa. They're sharing memories. And that is comforting."

"But he's dead. They're supposed to be sad."

Mom sighed. "There was a lot of sadness at the service, Michael. And I'm sure they'll feel sad later. But a person shouldn't stay sad all the time. Grandpa wouldn't want that." She reached out to smooth his hair. "Now come on."

He didn't move.

An "I mean it" look came into her eyes. "Michael, I'm not giving you a choice this time." She opened the door and stood waiting.

So he went in and sat down on the couch next to Mom. He did what she wanted. He listened to stories, he smiled when others laughed, and he replied when someone spoke to him. And inside, he ached. Maybe talking about Grandpa was comforting to everyone else, but not to him. After a while, he just couldn't listen anymore.

Faking hiccups, he excused himself to the kitchen for a glass of water.

At last, people began to trickle out the door. When they had all left, including Uncle Paul and his family, Mom and Dad went upstairs and Grandma went out to the porch. Jamie and Molly followed her.

Should he go after them, try to haul them away from her? He decided not to—he didn't want to risk upsetting Grandma. Instead, he began clearing off the table. Back and forth he went, from the dining room to the kitchen, back and forth, not having to think, just putting one foot in front of the other.

As he stood before the open refrigerator, trying to make room for all the leftovers, Dad came into the kitchen. "Mom's going to lie down for a while," he said. "She's pretty wrung out."

"Uh-huh."

"Feel like talking?"

Michael shook his head.

"Okay," Dad said. "In that case, I'll go check on Grandma and the girls."

Michael put the last of the food in the refrigerator, then headed upstairs, where he could go into his room and close the door. As he went past Mom and Dad's room, he stopped. Mom was crying. Of course she was. They'd just buried her dad. A sudden wave of guilt washed over him. Had he made it worse?

He hadn't meant to make her cry.

How many times had she sat with him when he was sick? She was always there when he needed her. There had to be something he could do for her now, something that would make her feel better. But what?

He went into the bathroom and soaked a washcloth in cold water. Then he squeezed it out and went back to Mom's door.

She was still sniffling. Should he bother her? He tried to push the door open quietly, but the old hinges squeaked. "Who's that?" she said, wiping her eyes with the edge of the pillowcase.

"Just me," Michael said. "I—I brought you this."

She took the cloth and put it across her eyes and forehead. A little smile appeared on her face. "That's nice," she said. "Thank you, Michael." She lay there without saying anything else.

"Mom?" Michael said at last. "I'm sorry if I made you feel bad."

She lifted the edge of the washcloth away from one eye. "You didn't," she said. "I guess the whole day just finally got to me."

"Do you need anything else?"

"Not right now."

"Okay." He turned to go. He was almost out the door when she said, "Michael?"

"Huh?"

"I really believe what I said—that Grandpa wouldn't want you to be sad all the time."

"I know." He closed the door behind him and leaned against it. He'd try. But the way he felt tonight, he couldn't imagine feeling anything else.

Five

Michael sat bolt upright in bed, breathless and shaking. The sun pouring in the window at the foot of the bed hurt his eyes, but for once he didn't care. After a night of tossing, turning, and awful dreams, it was finally morning.

When his heart stopped pounding he slid out of bed. The bare wood floor felt cool and solid and real under his feet. He pulled on some clothes, then stumbled toward the bathroom, where he splashed cold water on his face until his cheeks were almost numb.

Everyone else was up. The clock on the desk at the foot of the stairs said nine-thirty. Next to the clock stood a framed photo of Grandpa with a big smile. A lump settled in Michael's stomach as he thought about not seeing that smile anymore. Then he remembered what Mom had said last night. She was right. Grandpa hated seeing sadness, and always did all he could to get people to smile. *Gotta be careful about that frown,* he'd said to Michael one time. *If the wind changes, your face'll stay that way.*

Now Michael had to smile, just thinking about that.

From the kitchen window he could see the girls helping Grandma hang clothes on the line. Mom was on the phone in the living room. "Okay," she said, "see you soon." She hung up the phone and came into the kitchen, saying, "Morning, sleepyhead."

"Morning," Michael said. "Who was that?"

"Uncle Paul. He's coming over in a while. So, how are you this morning?"

"Okay. Still waking up. Where's Dad?"

"He went for a walk." She handed him a bowl and a box of cereal. "Here—have your breakfast. I'm going out to see if Grandma needs a hand."

"Mom," Michael said, "is Grandma all right?"

Mom paused with her hand on the doorknob. "Why do you ask that?"

"She seems to just go on the way she always does. I mean, except for the other day at the funeral home, she hasn't cried or anything."

"She cries, Michael. She just does it when she's alone. The rest of the time it's business as usual. It's her way—always has been." She opened the door. "Everyone deals with things differently, Michael. But we all have to deal with them."

Michael poured some cereal, wishing he could get his dreams out of his mind. He took a bite, but when he swallowed it seemed to stick in his throat. So did the next one. Finally he got up and dumped the rest into the cats' bowl. Maybe they would eat it.

As he was washing his bowl, he heard a car pulling

into the driveway. He peeked out the window and saw Uncle Paul getting out of his dark green pickup truck. With him was his grown stepson, Rick. Both were tall, good-natured men, tan from working outside. They had come to bale some hay Grandpa had raked the day before he died.

Uncle Paul had walked over to the field to take a look at it yesterday. Michael had heard him talking to Grandma. "The hay's still dry," he said, "but it shouldn't sit there much longer or it'll start to mildew. Rick and I will take care of it in the morning."

They came into the kitchen now with Grandma and Mom. "Sit a minute," Grandma was saying. "Do you want some coffee?"

"No, thanks," Uncle Paul said. "That part for the combine came in, and we've got some baling of our own to do, so I want to get this job done."

"I'll help," Michael said. "Could I drive the tractor?"

Uncle Paul shook his head. "I don't think so, Michael. Not today."

"Why not?"

"Because today I'd rather do it myself."

"But I know how," Michael persisted. "I did it a lot last year, with Grandpa."

"Yes, last year," Uncle Paul said. "And I don't have the time today to spend getting you reacquainted with it. Tell you what, though—Rick could probably use your help on the wagon."

Rick cocked his head, his eyes twinkling. "I don't know, Dad. He looks kind of puny."

Michael bristled. "I'm strong enough. But I don't want to stack bales. Grandpa promised me I could drive this year."

"Look, Michael," Uncle Paul said, "I'm sorry. I really don't want to argue about it anymore. The wagon will have to do for today."

"But that's not fair. That's not what Grandpa said I could do."

"Well, I'm not your grandpa."

"You sure aren't!"

"Michael Delaney!" Mom said. "You apologize to your uncle this minute!"

Michael met her eyes and looked away. "Sorry," he muttered.

"I guess we'll be getting to work, then," Uncle Paul said after an uncomfortable silence.

"What in the world got into you?" Mom asked after the men had gone back outside.

Michael shrugged his shoulders.

"Michael," Grandma said, "if you're not going to help them, would you take Jamie and Molly to pick raspberries for me? The fall reds are coming on early."

Don't argue, Mom's glance warned as he opened his mouth to protest.

"Sure, Grandma," he said, defeated.

Mom opened the kitchen door. "Girls," she called.

Jamie and Molly clattered up the steps and into the kitchen, looking like scarecrows in their grubby clothes and beat-up old straw hats. "We're ready," Molly said.

"Where are the baskets?" Jamie asked.

"Right here," Mom said. "Now remember: get all the ripe ones, even the littlest ones. But before you go, you need to put on sunblock."

She took a tube from the windowsill over the sink and squeezed some of the thick white cream into Jamie's outstretched hands. "You, too, Molly," she said, squeezing some into her own hands and rubbing it onto Molly's arms and face. "Here." She gave Michael the tube. "Don't forget your neck and the tops of your ears."

Michael smeared on the sunblock, then took his Yankees cap from a hook by the refrigerator. "Okay," he said, "let's go."

The girls frisked around Michael like a couple of puppies as they started down the driveway. "Have fun," Mom called out the kitchen window.

Fun? By the time they were finished, Michael's back ached and his hands were covered with scratches from the thorny raspberry bushes. He and the girls took the berries, four quarts, into the kitchen. Uncle Paul and Rick had finished baling and were sitting there talking with Mom and Dad and Grandma.

"Done?" Grandma asked. "Goodness, child," she said to Molly, laughing at the sight of the girl's red-stained face, "did you get any in a basket?"

"You look a little warm, son," Uncle Paul said to Michael. "How about going fishing this evening with your cousin and me?"

Michael shook his head. "No, thanks."

"You sure? Some time with your rod and reel might do you good."

"I don't want to." Michael left the kitchen, headed for the porch.

"Hey!" Dad said. "Get back here!"

"I'm sorry, Paul," Michael heard Mom say. "He's really upset right now. He's not usually like this."

Michael let the porch door slam and headed straight for the cherry tree in the front yard. He began to climb, his feet finding a set of natural steps formed by some big old knots. Up he went until he reached the fork he used to call his spy seat, from where he could see the road, the driveway, and much of the yard.

As he settled in, he heard voices in the driveway. Uncle Paul and Rick, going home. "I don't care if she is my sister," Uncle Paul said as they reached their pickup truck. "She needs to take care of that kid's attitude. And his mouth. Doesn't he know we're all upset?"

The words stung. Michael knew Uncle Paul had just wanted to help him feel better. But fishing was something special between him and Grandpa. He wasn't ready to share that with anyone else. Not yet.

The porch door squeaked open and slapped shut.

Michael peered down through the leaves. Mom. She walked across the grass in bare feet, carrying a glass of iced tea, and settled into a long lawn chair beneath the cherry tree.

Great. It looked like he was going to be up here for a while. But wait. She was leaning her head back and closing her eyes. Maybe she'd fall asleep, and then he could climb down without being noticed.

It might have worked if a robin hadn't decided it didn't like where he was sitting. It perched on a nearby branch saying, "Cheep, cheep." After a few minutes of this, Mom opened one eye and looked up. "So there you are," she said, opening the other eye. "I wondered where you'd gone."

"Cheep, cheep," the robin said, more and more insistent.

"That bird sounds really upset," Mom said. "Maybe you'd better come down."

"I'm not going to bother it."

"I know that, Michael, and so do you, but the bird obviously doesn't. Anyway, we need to talk."

There was no way out. Michael slithered down the tree trunk and stood in front of Mom's chair, brushing bits of bark off his shirt. "What?"

"Why don't you get a chair," she said.

He pulled one over from under the maple tree, and they sat in silence for a few minutes. Michael swatted at a couple of mosquitoes buzzing around his head. "They're bad today, aren't they?" Mom said, slapping at her leg.

"It's because the air is so still," Michael said.

"I remember one summer when I was a little older than you," Mom said. "The mosquitoes were so big, Grandpa said he was sure someone had crossed them with hummingbirds." She smiled. "He hated mosquitoes. But oh, how they loved him."

Michael smiled and brushed an ant off the arm of his chair.

"You and Grandpa had big plans, didn't you?"

"Yeah. That's why he and Grandma gave me that fishing rod for my birthday."

"You were way out of line with Uncle Paul, you know."

"I couldn't help it, Mom. He and Rick made me so mad. They've seen me work. Heck, Uncle Paul's even seen me drive. They were just jerking me around. It wasn't fair."

She nodded. "Perhaps. But even so . . ." Her voice trailed off. She took a long swallow of her tea. "Dad's going back tomorrow."

"I know."

"He and I have been talking, and we think it might be best for you and the girls to go back with him."

She wasn't serious. She couldn't be.

But everything—her voice, her eyes—said she was.

"What about you, Mom?"

"I'm going to stay here with Grandma for a bit."

"Why do you get to stay?"

"Because she's my mother, Michael." She bit her lower lip and looked away. When she spoke again, her voice was gentler. "You asked earlier if Grandma was all right. Well, she isn't, not really. She just lost the person who's been the main part of her life for over fifty years. She needs some quiet and calm right now, and—"

"Mom, listen—I said I was sorry for what I said. I won't do it again. I promise."

"I believe you, Michael. Still, it's not just that. It's all the tension around here. You, me, Dad—even the girls have been cranky. It's just not good for Grandma."

She was right. Deep inside, Michael knew she was right. And he didn't want to make things bad for Grandma. Still, the words spilled out of him. "You think that's going to change if we go home? I'll be the one stuck with their crankiness most of the time, because Dad'll be holed up at the university like he's been all summer."

"No, you won't. He'll be working at home more than he has been. Mrs. Jackson will be coming over on the weekdays to help out when he's not there. And school starts in a couple of weeks. I'll be home before then."

So it was all arranged. He squeezed his eyes shut so tight they hurt. When he opened them, all he said was, "It's not fair."

"Michael," Mom said, throwing her hands up, "will you listen to yourself. 'It's not fair, it's not fair,' as if all that's been happening is a conspiracy against you personally. Well, it's not. It's just life. And, as Grandpa used to say, 'In life, fair has nothing to do with it.' "

Michael got up and started walking across the yard. He heard Mom say, "Michael, come back," but instead he broke into a slow, steady run. Across the road he went and down the lane, running until a pain in his side made him stop, the first real pain he'd allowed himself to feel in days. Mom was right about one thing, he thought as he caught his breath. Fair had nothing to do with any of this. And that was the most unfair thing of all.

SIX

As Michael carried his duffel bag down the narrow staircase after breakfast, he could hear Mom and Grandma in the kitchen, talking as they did the breakfast dishes. Jamie and Molly sat in the middle of the living room floor, building a castle out of dominoes.

"Be careful," Jamie said as he walked by.

"I am," he said, hoisting his bag up onto his shoulder. He tiptoed past them and had stopped a safe distance away when Jamie yelled, "Timber!" and the castle fell with a clatter.

Michael thunked his bag onto the floor. "Why'd you do that after telling me to be so careful?"

Jamie grinned. " 'Cause I wanted to knock it down myself."

"Pssh." Michael shook his head and went into the kitchen.

"There you are," Mom said. "Good. Dad's putting stuff in the car, so you'd better take that out to him."

Michael went out the kitchen door, and through the garage, and put his bag in the driveway where Dad would see it. Then he jogged across the road to the hay barn.

The faded red tractor stood in the wide doorway, half in and half out. Michael reached up and thumped his hand against the hard rubber tires, warm from the morning sun, then walked past it into the dim, cavelike barn.

The still air smelled of dust and old hay and diesel fuel. A barn swallow swooped in over his head, circled once, and dove back out into the bright morning light.

He climbed onto the tractor and sat in the driver's seat. Gripping the steering wheel, he closed his eyes, remembering last summer when he'd sat here in front of Grandpa. He'd handled the steering wheel, but his legs had been too short to reach the pedals, so Grandpa had worked those. *Don't you worry 'bout that, Mickey,* Grandpa had said. *My guess is that you're going to do some growing over the winter. By next summer, you'll reach those pedals just fine.* Now he stretched his legs forward. Grandpa had been right.

"Michael?"

Michael's eyes snapped open. Uncle Paul stood looking up at him.

"What're you doing up there, boy?"

Michael stared at the steering wheel. "Thinking."

"This is a good place for that," Uncle Paul said. "Used to come here myself sometimes when I was your age." He reached up and took a pair of leather gloves from the transmission cover in front of the seat. "Today I just came by to get these. I left them here yesterday."

Michael didn't say anything.

Uncle Paul patted the gloves. "Yep—they're my best ones. I'd hate to lose 'em."

Michael looked toward him and nodded, avoiding his eyes.

Uncle Paul pulled a faded bandanna out of his back pocket and wiped his neck. "Well, I guess I'll be going." He turned to leave.

"Uncle Paul—wait." Michael jumped to the ground. The big man turned to face him.

"About yesterday. I'm . . . I'm sorry."

"Apology accepted, Michael," Uncle Paul said after a moment. He held out his hand—a hand that was tanned and roughened by weather and work. A hand very much like Grandpa's. Michael stretched his lighter, smoother one out and gripped it.

As they stood looking at each other, there was a shrill whistle outside and the blare of a car horn.

"That's Dad," Michael said. "I think he's calling me."

Uncle Paul gave his hand a firm squeeze. "We'll be seeing you," he said. He slapped the tractor. "This'll be here next time you come."

Michael crossed the yard, dodging a cat that streaked past him with something in its mouth. As he passed the pump in the side yard, he stopped. Years ago, when he was just a little kid, he'd asked Grandpa why the pump handle went around and around, instead of up and down. Grandpa had just laughed. *Well, Mickey, some go up and down, some go around. Either way, you get your water.*

Dad could wait a couple of minutes. Taking the old

metal cup off its hook, Michael cranked the pump's handle. Icy water gushed out the spigot, filling the cup, spilling over the edge onto the grass. He gulped the water, cold and tinny-tasting. *That's as good as it gets,* he could hear Grandpa say. He smiled and cranked himself another cup. "You said it, Grandpa," he whispered, and drained the cup in one long swallow.

"Michael!" Molly stood by the corner of the house. "Daddy says come on!"

Michael waved to show he'd heard. He hung the cup back on its hook, remembering the day he'd shown Molly how to work the pump. "It's magic!" she'd said. She'd turned the handle again and again, until her sneakers were soaked.

One more time, he cranked the handle, stretching his left hand out beneath the sudden whoosh of water. Then he wiped his hand on his jeans and walked around the house to the driveway.

Mom and Dad stood next to Dad's car. "Everything's loaded," Dad said.

"Grandma wants to see you inside," Mom said.

Michael pushed open the kitchen door. "Grandma?" he called.

"Right here." Grandma came in from the living room. She held a small jeweler's-type box and something flat, wrapped in wrinkled white tissue paper. "I wanted to give you these."

Michael took the box, its black velvet worn smooth from years of opening and closing, and opened it. Inside lay a tiny pewter largemouth bass that looked real enough to take a hook. Grandpa's favorite tie tack. Swallowing hard, he peeled the tissue paper away from the other item, revealing the photo of him and Grandpa with the big fish, in a small wooden frame.

He could hardly get the words past the lump in his throat. "Grandma," he said, holding the frame and the box out, "you should keep these."

She put her hands on his and shook her head. "He was planning to give them to you, Michael."

Michael hugged Grandma, biting his lower lip. If he started to cry, so would she, and that was something he just couldn't handle.

Grandma gave him one last pat on the back and kissed his cheek. "Time for you to get going, I guess," she said. Together they went outside.

While Grandma kissed Dad and the girls goodbye, Michael tried one last time. "Please, Mom, can't I stay?"

She shook her head. "Not this time, Michael." She hugged him. "Help Dad and Mrs. Jackson, okay?"

"Okay."

"Michael." Mom cupped his cheek in her hand and leaned forward to kiss him. "I love you."

"You, too." He pulled away and got into the front seat.

The girls climbed in back, and Dad got in and started the engine. "I'll call you tonight," he said to Mom.

As the car left the driveway, Michael stared out the side window. Tears oozed from the corners of his eyes and trickled down his face as they passed the potato field and the horse barn, rounded the curve, and headed onto the main road.

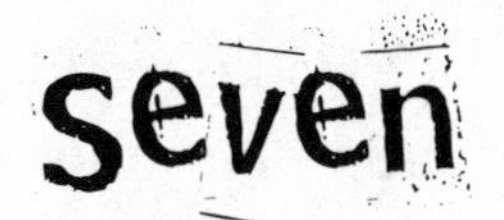

Michael looked at his watch. Quarter to three. Late enough to consider today pretty much gone. With a red marker, he crossed the date off the *Lord of the Rings* wall calendar hanging over his desk.

August 13.

Eleven days since Grandpa died.

A week since he'd come home with Dad and the girls.

All during that week, Dad had spent most of his time on his dissertation. Jamie and Molly played with each other or their friends. For them, things were the same as always.

But not for him.

He tried. He read. He played Battleship, pinball, and Starfighter on the computer. He wished he could surf the Net, but Mom and Dad had put parental controls on the server, so he couldn't do much there. He tried to watch TV, but Mrs. Jackson made him turn it off.

"Not when the weather's so nice," she'd said. "You should be outside with your friends."

"T.J. won't be home from camp for another week," he said, "and Brad's still at the shore. There's nothing to do by myself."

"I'll find you something," she said.

Next thing he knew, he'd been sweeping the patio.

He flopped backward onto his bed. This wasn't how these days were supposed to be.

"I might as well be in solitary," he grumbled.

He rolled over and buried his face in his pillow. Reaching out, he groped for the ON button of his CD player. But he missed, and his hand hit the framed photo Grandma had given him. It fell over with a clunk.

Sitting up, he righted it. As he looked at it, he could hear Grandpa saying, *You're turning into a real good fisherman, Mickey. Good thing, too—the family reputation will be safe with you after I'm gone.*

He turned the CD player on. U2's *Joshua Tree.* He closed his eyes, letting the first song's opening wash over him, chords that sounded like church music. A guitar crept in, followed by the steady beat of a drum and a bass line he could feel thrumming through him. He pushed the volume up, letting Bono's rough wailing, "I want to run, I want to hide . . ." fill the room.

A few minutes later, there was a pounding on his door. It was Mrs. Jackson, with a smudge of flour on her face and fire in her eyes. "I can hear that above Molly's chatter *and* the mixer," she said. "Would you turn it down before the neighbors start calling?"

"Sure," he said. "Sorry." He closed the door again.

Jeez—sometimes she could be so bossy. He turned the volume down and put on his headphones.

He picked up his sketch pad and a pencil. Dad had told him once that if someone made you mad, it helped to imagine them in a suit of long underwear. The pencil began to move, slowly at first, then more and more quickly. In a few minutes, he had a caricature of Mrs. Jackson from the rear, her broad back end looking even bigger than usual.

He had to smile. Dad was right. It worked.

That was the last page on the pad. He jumped up. That's what he could do—ride his bike over to Miller's Art Supplies for a new one.

He grabbed his wallet from his desk and opened it. "Aw, man," he said, tossing it back. Not anywhere near enough. Mom hadn't given him this month's allowance.

He'd ask Dad tonight.

But when dinnertime came, Dad was preoccupied. He kept staring off at nothing, with what Mom called "that space cadet look" in his eyes.

"Earth to Dad," Michael said with a grin.

Dad blinked. "Sorry," he said. "I guess I was writing in my head." He chuckled. "I don't know why ideas come to me so often during dinner."

Michael thought for a moment. "Maybe they're just something else to chew on?"

Jamie giggled.

"What's funny?" Molly asked.

Dad shook his head. "Michael, I think you've inherited Grandpa's love of bad jokes."

Michael thought about all the times he'd groaned when Grandpa was being funny. A lump formed in his stomach, and he couldn't eat anything else. He just pushed the food around on his plate while Dad thought some more and Jamie and Molly cleaned their plates.

When the girls had finished and left the table, Michael said, "Dad, can I have this month's allowance?"

Dad looked at him, but didn't seem to have heard.

"I need a new sketch pad," Michael said. "I have some money, but not enough."

Dad blinked and was back on earth again. "Sketch pad?"

"Yeah. About this big—lots of blank paper—used for drawing?"

Dad nodded. "I know what a sketch pad is, Michael." He opened his wallet. "You'll have to wait until tomorrow," he said. "I need to go to the ATM. I can give it to you when I get home."

"Couldn't you go tonight?"

"Sorry," Dad said, "not tonight. I'm tired, and I don't feel like going out. Why don't you take a few sheets of paper out of the printer in Mom's office. I'm sure she wouldn't mind."

"That's okay. I'll wait." Michael pushed his chair away from the table. "Can I be excused?"

"Not yet. I want to talk to you about something."

That didn't sound good. "What?"

"I was wondering if you'd like to try some art lessons?"

"Art lessons?"

"Art lessons. I stopped at the library on my way home, and while I was there, I ran into a friend I haven't seen in years, a guy named Charles Andrews. He taught art at the high school when I first started teaching. We got talking, and I told him about you and your drawing."

"What'd you tell him?"

"That you always seem to have a pencil in your hand. And about the prize you won last year. Is that okay?"

Michael's ears felt warm. "Yeah."

"Anyway," Dad said, "he's been needing someone to help him with yard work. He said if you'd be interested in putting in some regular time doing that, he'd give you lessons in exchange."

Michael frowned. "What's he like?"

"He's a good man," Dad said, "and a talented artist."

"Where does he live?"

"Just over on Maple Street. You could ride your bike."

"I don't know," Michael said. "Can I think about it?"

"Sure. I just thought it was something you might enjoy. And I know how much you've been missing Grandpa. I thought this might help."

A question popped into Michael's head. He tried to ignore it, but it had to be asked. "You aren't expecting him to take Grandpa's place, are you?"

Dad stood up. "Michael," he said, "I just don't know what to say anymore. Sometimes it seems that whatever I say is the wrong thing. I've told you my reasons. You think about it and let me know what you decide."

Michael stared at his knees. Dad had seemed really

excited about this. And real art lessons from a teacher outside of school was something he'd thought about for a long time. "I guess I could give it a try," he said.

Dad handed him a piece of paper. "Here's his number. Go give him a call."

"Now?"

"Why not?"

Michael went into the kitchen and started to dial the number Dad had given him. Halfway through, he stopped and hung up. How could he talk with his mouth so dry? "Just do it," he said to himself, picking up the receiver and dialing again.

After a couple of rings, a deep voice said, "Hello?"

Michael swallowed hard. "Uh, hi. This is Michael Delaney."

"Michael," the voice at the other end said. "Have you decided to take me up on my offer?"

"Yes."

"Great. What do you think about this Saturday for getting started?"

"All right, I guess."

"You know where I live?"

"Somewhere on Maple."

"Number 456, to be exact. Nine o'clock?"

"Sure."

"Fine. I'll see you then."

Michael hung up the phone and went back to his room. Mr. Andrews sounded okay.

But like the guy? He wasn't making any promises.

Eight

"You stupid . . ." Michael gave the stalled mower a shove with his foot. How old was this thing, and when was the last time it had a tune-up? He must have restarted it nine or ten times in the past couple of hours.

He pulled out the bandanna he'd stuffed into his pocket and wiped his forehead and neck. Time to take a break.

Mr. Andrews had left a glass and an insulated jug filled with lemonade on the back porch. Michael filled the glass to the rim, then took a huge gulp that washed down his throat and sloshed against the wall of his stomach. Man, that was good. He pressed the glass against his face, letting cold drops of condensation trickle down his cheek. Sighing, he drank the rest of the glass and stretched. "Okay," he said through clenched teeth as he returned to the mower and pulled the starter cord. "You'd better behave."

As if it had understood what he said, the machine started right up. He finished mowing, then used the trimmer around the edges of the gardens and along the sidewalk.

Finally, he was finished. Mr. Andrews had better teach him something worth the grief that mower had given him.

He put the mower and the trimmer in the garage, then went up on the back porch and knocked on the screen door. No answer. He knocked again, louder. "Mr. Andrews?"

"Door's open." The voice came out the kitchen window.

Michael went in. At the sight of the cabinets on the far wall, he stopped and stared. The outsides of the cabinets weren't anything special, just glossy white enamel. But the insides, visible through glass doors, were another story. Each one was painted a different color—lime green, sunflower yellow, cherry red, and more. After a couple of minutes, his eyes felt as if they were beginning to vibrate.

He heard a chuckle. He looked toward the stove and saw Mr. Andrews standing there with a mug in his hand.

"Want some coffee?" he said. "It's just instant, but I think it's pretty good."

"No, thanks," Michael said. "I don't drink it."

"Lemonade?"

"That's okay. I had some while I was working."

Mr. Andrews came over to stand beside Michael. "So, what do you think?"

"It's kind of a cool idea," Michael said.

"But—"

Michael looked at the man. "But what?"

"I heard some hesitation in your voice." Mr. Andrews took a sip of coffee. "Come on, you don't have to be polite. Tell me what you think."

Michael swallowed. "I like the idea. But"—he frowned—"it's just so . . . so random. It feels like it's too much."

"How would you have done it?"

"Fewer colors. Maybe just one or two, but different shades. Some light, some dark."

"Go on."

"Or, if you wanted more colors, you could do something with the spectrum." He pointed to the center cabinet. "You could start here, with red, then put orange on either side, then yellow, and so on. Or maybe use purple over there and go across the wall, ending with red."

Mr. Andrews nodded. "Interesting." He studied the cabinets, as if picturing Michael's suggestions. "You have a good eye."

He took another swig of his coffee and set the mug in the sink. "Come on, I'll show you my studio.

"It's nice to have a little company now and then," he continued as they went into the front part of the house. "I usually rattle around this place alone."

They went through the dining room, past a corner cupboard filled with glasses, china, and lots of odds and ends. Just like the cupboard in Grandma's dining room.

A painting in the front hall caught Michael's eye, a watercolor of autumn trees.

Mr. Andrews, already on his way up the stairs, said,

"Take a few minutes to look at it if you want. I'll be in the studio."

Michael leaned close to the painting. There were so many different shades of orange and red and yellow and brown. He took a step back, and another. As he did, the brushstrokes softened and blended together.

He had backed all the way into the living room. Over the mantel hung a painting of a woman with dark hair. Framed photographs were everywhere, and shelves on either side of the fireplace were as full as the cupboard in the dining room.

He remembered a conversation from when he was Jamie's age, as he and Grandpa stood in front of Grandma's dining room cupboard.

"Grandpa, what is all this stuff?"

"Well, let's see. We bought that bowl on our honeymoon. The blue-and-white plate belonged to my great-grandmother. And you gave that little china camel to Grandma."

"I remember. It was in a box of tea bags."

"I guess you could say these are all memories you can touch, Mickey. They're all reminders of people and places that have been special to us."

"Michael?" Mr. Andrews called.

"Coming." Michael took the stairs two at a time. At the top, he looked around. Now where?

"In here." The voice came from a room down the hall.

Michael paused in the doorway. Mr. Andrews stood at a table with a slanted top in the middle of the room, a long, thin brush in his hand.

Michael looked around the studio. At first, it seemed as cluttered as the rest of the house. But the longer he looked, the more organization he saw. On one wall, a large piece of Peg-Board held racks for brushes arranged by size. Beneath the Peg-Board stood three eight-drawer organizers with labels on each drawer. Sketch pads, notebooks, canvas stretchers, and a roll of canvas lay on shelves on the opposite wall. On either side of the window, bookshelves stretched from floor to ceiling.

On the slanted table lay a watercolor of an old building and trees reflected in still water. "I know where that is," Michael said. "It's up by the reservoir."

"Sure is."

A larger painting of snow-covered pine trees leaned against the wall beneath the Peg-Board. It looked real. Not photograph-real, but real the way Michael remembered winter. As he looked at it, he actually shivered.

He wanted to be this good.

"Do you draw or paint?" Mr. Andrews asked.

"Draw, mostly. We've done some painting in school, but not much."

"What kind of drawing do you like to do?"

"I'm pretty good at perspective and animals. I haven't done much with landscapes, though." He looked over at the painting on the table. "I'd like to try."

Mr. Andrews scratched his head. "I realized while you were outside that I forgot to ask you to bring some of your work with you this morning."

"Why?"

"Before I can begin to teach you, I need to see what you can already do." He went to the shelves and pulled out a book. "This is one of my favorites on landscapes. Take it home and read it."

"That's it?" All that work, and he was just supposed to read?

"I'm afraid so." Mr. Andrews rubbed the sides of his forehead. "I woke up with a headache that I just can't seem to shake. I promise you, though, next week we'll get cracking. Okay?"

"Sure." *Whatever.*

"Do you believe me?"

No grownup had ever asked him that before. "I guess."

"Good. I may tick you off once in a while, Michael, but I will never lie to you. Got that?"

Michael nodded.

"All right. See you next week, then."

When Michael got home, the smell of fresh-cut grass was in the air. Dad had been mowing, too. Maybe they could go over to the park and play some basketball after lunch.

Dad was in the kitchen, his hair still damp from the shower, making a peanut butter sandwich. "Hey," he said. "How'd it go?"

"Okay, I guess. Want to go shoot some baskets?"

"Sorry. Not today. Now that you're home, I have to go down to school. I ran into a snag with a program and I want to get it straightened out."

"Can't you do it Monday?"

"No. I want to get it done now. The regular students come back in a few days, which means it'll be harder to get time in the computer lab." He put the sandwich in a plastic bag. "So, what did you do this morning?"

"I cut the grass. But he didn't give me a lesson."

"Why not?"

"He forgot to tell me that he wants to see some of my work first. And he had a headache. He told me to read this instead." Michael tossed the book on the kitchen table.

"Hey," Dad said. "I know you're disappointed, but this was only your first day. He's a great guy."

"Right."

"Just give him a chance, Michael, okay?"

"Why?"

"Because I'm asking you to."

Michael thought about this. Then, raising an eyebrow, he asked, "You really were good friends?"

"Yes. He helped me learn the ropes when I started teaching."

"What happened?"

"What do you mean?"

"I've never heard you talk about him. Did you have a fight or something?"

"Of course not." Dad put the sandwich into his battered briefcase. "He retired, and I didn't see him as often."

"Why not?"

"I had things to do. My job, the family. It just got

harder to find the time. That happens, Michael. Sometimes people just drift apart."

Kind of like us.

For a moment, neither of them said anything. Then Dad broke the silence. "I'd better get going. The girls already had lunch—they're playing next door. I'll be home to fix dinner." He shook his head. "I'll be glad when Mom gets home on Thursday. Her cooking is so much better than mine."

"You can say that again."

"Just for that, you can vacuum the downstairs." He picked up his briefcase and went out the door.

Michael sat there for a while, thinking about what Dad had said. People drifting apart when they didn't see each other. Maybe he had something in common with Mr. Andrews besides art.

Michael sat on his bed, surrounded by drawings he'd done in school last year. He'd been trying for almost an hour to decide what to take to show Mr. Andrews, and nothing seemed good enough.

He'd never been afraid to let a teacher see what he'd drawn. He hardly knew Mr. Andrews—why should he be so concerned about what the old guy thought? But every time he thought about that snow painting, and about how it had made him feel, he knew why.

He opened his sketch pad. All week he'd been studying Mr. Andrews's book. Toward the end of the week, he'd decided to try copying a couple of the landscapes in the book. But they didn't look quite right, and he couldn't figure out why.

What was it Grandpa had said once? *If you know where you're having trouble, Mickey, seems to me that's the place to start working.*

He'd take the sketch pad.

He had to get moving, or he'd be late. He grabbed

his backpack and Mr. Andrews's book and went downstairs for breakfast.

Mom and Dad weren't up yet. Now that Jamie was old enough to make a toast and cereal kind of breakfast for herself and Molly, they slept in a little on the weekends.

He dumped his things on the kitchen table. "Budge over," he said to Jamie, who was at the counter, buttering toast. "I've got to be there in twenty minutes."

Jamie stayed put, so he reached into a cupboard above her head and took out a box of cereal. He shook it. Just enough for one bowl. He started to pour.

"Hey," Jamie said. "I wanted that."

"Too bad," he said. "Molly, *no*!"

He dropped the box and lunged toward the table, where Molly was reaching for Mr. Andrews's book with buttery fingers. He snatched the book up and hugged it to his chest. "Jeez, Molly, mess up your own stuff. This isn't even mine." He checked the cover for butter stains, then slid the book into his backpack.

Molly's lower lip began to quiver.

"Talk about messes," Jamie said. "Look what you did, Michael."

"Shut up, Jamie." Tiny *o*'s littered the counter and the floor. Sighing, Michael got the broom and dustpan. He was going to be late. There was no way around it. While he swept, Jamie brushed the cereal on the counter into a bowl.

"I got it after all," she said.

"Who cares?" Michael put the broom and dustpan

away, gulped a glass of juice, and grabbed some cookies from the jar on the counter. "I've got to go."

"I'm telling Mom you ate cookies for breakfast," Jamie said.

"Don't wake her up. Anyway, it's okay. They're oatmeal." Michael banged the door as he went out. "Sisters," he muttered as he got on his bike and took off down the driveway.

When he reached Mr. Andrews's house, he leaned his bike against the back porch and knocked on the screen door.

Nothing.

"Mr. Andrews?" he called.

He tried the door. It was open. He stepped inside.

From somewhere inside, he heard music followed by a loud laugh. Mr. Andrews must have the TV or the radio on and hadn't heard him knock.

Michael put his backpack on the kitchen table. From the direction of the living room, he heard a familiar "Beep! Beep!"

The Road Runner? Michael headed for the living room, reaching the doorway just as a boulder landed on Wile E. Coyote.

"Morning," Mr. Andrews said. "You'd think that critter'd learn after a while."

"Yeah," Michael said. The guy was watching cartoons? At his age?

"You're never too old for some things," Mr. Andrews said, almost as if he could read Michael's mind.

"I guess not," Michael said. He winced as the coyote

dropped off a cliff. "So, what do you want me to do today?"

Mr. Andrews picked up the remote control and muted the volume. "It's been dry enough that the grass doesn't need cutting. Have you ever done any hedge trimming?"

"Once."

"Great. The front and side hedges have gotten kind of shaggy. You don't have to trim them a lot, just get rid of the pieces that stick out like hair first thing in the morning. The bushes aren't too high, or too wide, so you shouldn't have any trouble reaching."

"That's it?"

"I think that'll be plenty. You'll find the clippers in the garage."

"Okay. Where do I plug them in?"

"You don't."

"Oh." Great. Another relic. This guy should start a museum. "Okay."

The hedge shears Michael found hanging on the garage wall were at least as old as the lawn mower, and their action was kind of stiff. He looked around and found a can of the stuff Dad used when the back door hinges squeaked, and gave the clippers a shot. Then he started on the bushes.

When he finally hung the shears back on their hook, the hedges were a little ragged in spots, but they looked better than they had. He stretched and rubbed his aching arms and shoulders, and went into the house.

He picked up his backpack as he went through the

kitchen. Stopping at the bottom of the hall stairs, he called, "Mr. Andrews?"

"Up here."

Mr. Andrews stood at his table, frowning at a watercolor of an old bridge. Michael came around to look. "That's the one north of town."

Mr. Andrews nodded. "But that spot there," he said, pointing. "It's not right." He reached for a short-bristled brush and dipped it in water.

What was he doing? "Wait," Michael said. "Don't wreck it."

Mr. Andrews smiled as he gently scrubbed with the brush on a small area of the paper. "Don't worry," he said. "Just watch."

Michael held his breath as Mr. Andrews blotted where he'd scrubbed. The paper was clean. Michael leaned forward to look at the paper. "I didn't know you could do that."

"You can if it's a small area," Mr. Andrews said. "Otherwise, you just have to start over."

Michael reached into his backpack. "Here's your book."

Mr. Andrews put the book in its place on the shelf. "How'd you like it?"

"It was good."

"So, did you bring me anything to look at?"

"Uh-huh." Michael took out his sketch pad, and handed it over.

Mr. Andrews began to flip through the pages, nodding. "Hmm." He paused at the sketch of the hay barn

Michael had done at the farm. "I like this one," he said. "Where is it?"

"At my grandparents' farm."

"What do you think of it?"

"The barn's okay, but I don't like the background."

"Why not?"

"It seems kind of stiff."

"As I said last week, you have a good eye." Mr. Andrews reached for some paper and a pencil lying on a nearby shelf and set them in front of Michael. "Here," he said, "do that section again." He watched Michael draw for a minute or two, then said, "Hold it."

Michael stopped. "What?"

"Two things. First, when I look at the drawing, do you want me to look at the barn or the background?"

"The barn."

"Then don't give me so many details in the background. That's where the cluttered feeling is coming from. Second, it looks stiff because your hand is stiff. You needed that tight control when you drew the barn, but this is different. You want it softer here. Keep your wrist loose."

He got up and walked around the table. Standing behind Michael, he picked up his forearm and shook it. "Relax," he said. Michael's hand began to flop. "That's right." He put a fresh sheet of paper on the table. "Now try."

Michael began to draw again.

"Use your whole arm," Mr. Andrews said. "There you go."

Michael smiled. "It's a lot better. Thanks."

They worked in silence for a while. When Michael finally put his pencil down and stretched his neck, Mr. Andrews said, "Let's see."

Michael held up both drawings.

Mr. Andrews nodded. "Very good, Michael. You really understood what I was talking about." He rinsed his brush in a plastic container of water, wiped it gently on a sponge, and rolled it to a point between his fingers. "Now, how about some cider? I got some yesterday, first of the season."

"I guess so." Michael packed up his things and followed him down the stairs. He waited in the living room while Mr. Andrews went to the kitchen and came back a few minutes later with two glasses of cider and a plate of cookies.

Michael took a sip of cider. Then he pointed to a photograph on top of the television. "Is that you?"

"Sure is," Mr. Andrews said. "With my wife, Lucy, and our daughter, Jean. Lucy died a few years ago, and Jean lives in Chicago. That's so far away. I miss her." He paused for a moment. "But I imagine you know about missing someone."

Michael stiffened. "What do you mean?"

"Your dad told me about your grandfather."

Michael looked away.

Mr. Andrews took another cookie. "School starts Wednesday?"

"Tuesday," Michael said, relieved that the subject had changed.

"Looking forward to it?"

Michael shrugged. "I guess so."

Mr. Andrews laughed. "With that expression you look just like your dad. I remember his first day of teaching. He acted so cool, sitting on the edge of his desk while he talked. Later, he told me his knees were so shaky he couldn't stand."

Michael tried to picture Dad that nervous.

"Anyway," Mr. Andrews continued, "by the end of the day the whole school knew that Mr. Delaney had stood up and gotten his foot stuck in the wastebasket in three different classes." He laughed harder. "It took him a long time to live that one down. And I don't think he ever sat on his desk again."

Michael smiled. Dad, stuck in a wastebasket?

"He settled down," Mr. Andrews finished, "and he was a damn good teacher." He took a sip of cider. "So, tell me, how's he doing now?"

"He's fine," Michael said.

"What kind of things do you two do together? I remember he was pretty good on the faculty basketball team."

"We play a little sometimes," Michael said. "But not much lately. He's been writing his Ph.D. dissertation."

Mr. Andrews nodded. "He mentioned that when we talked. He must be pretty busy."

"Yeah. He is." Michael looked at his watch. "Is there anything else you want me to do today?"

"Wasn't the hedge trimming enough?"

Michael rubbed the blister on his palm and nodded.

"Then I think we're done for the day. Why don't you choose a couple of sketches in your book and redo them this week, remembering to keep your arm loose."

"Okay." Michael picked up his backpack. "See you next week."

As he rode up his driveway, a basketball came flying from behind him, hit the garage, and bounced into the bushes. He screeched to a stop, dropped his bike, and retrieved the ball. There was nobody in sight.

"All right," he said. "Where are you?"

Silence.

"T.J., I know you're there. Your initials are on the ball. Come on out."

There was a rustle in the branches of the tree alongside the driveway. A pair of sneakers appeared, followed by long denim-covered legs. "Look out below," a voice said, and T.J. dropped to the ground.

He brushed a couple of leaves from his sandy hair, adjusted his glasses, and grinned at Michael. "I'm ba-a-ack."

"I can see that," Michael said. "When'd you get home?"

"Last night."

"How was camp?"

"Same old stuff. It'll be better next year, when I'm a junior counselor. Then I can tell the little kids what to do."

"Is Brad back?"

"Yeah. We're going over to the school to shoot some baskets. Want to come?"

"I don't know. I'm kind of tired."

T.J. began bouncing the basketball. "Yeah, when I got here, your mom said you were working. Where'd you get a job?"

"I'm doing some stuff for a friend of my dad's. It's nothing major."

"Oh. Well, how was the farm this year? Did you catch any big fish?"

Michael shook his head.

T.J. bounced the ball to Michael. "Aw, come on, what are we talking? Three feet? Four?"

Michael stood there, keeping his eyes on the ball as it bounced back and forth, each bounce a little higher. "I didn't get any."

"You and your grandpa, the world's greatest fishermen, didn't catch anything at all? What happened, did the pond dry up?"

Michael bounced the ball hard, sending it back to T.J. "Grandpa died. I had a rotten time. I've spent a big chunk of last Saturday and today working for this Andrews guy, and my arms are killing me because he has antique hedge cutters. Any more questions?"

T.J. stood there with his mouth open.

"Sorry," Michael said. "I just don't want to talk about it. Okay?"

"Sure. Whatever." T.J. was trying not to sound hurt, but Michael knew him too well.

Michael picked up his bike. "I've got to go. See you later." He left T.J. in the driveway and put his bike in the garage.

He went inside and headed straight to his room, shutting the door. As he looked at the photo of Grandpa on the nightstand he could hear Mr. Andrews say, *You know about missing someone.*

It was as if the guy could see right into him and know what he thought.

Michael lay back and closed his eyes, stretching and relaxing the muscles in his arms. As he lay there, he could suddenly hear Grandpa's voice. *You have to give people a chance, Mickey. Sometimes it's hard. Sometimes you don't want to. Once in a while you might be disappointed, but most of the time it's worth the effort.*

Okay. He'd give Mr. Andrews a chance.

He just hoped this wouldn't be a "once in a while."

Ten

"Michael, aren't you ready yet? You don't want to be late the first day!"

"Okay, Mom." Michael bounded down the stairs and into the kitchen. He wolfed down his breakfast while Mom fussed with Jamie's hair.

"Dad was sorry he didn't get to see you before he left for work," Mom said. "He said for you to have a good day."

"Is kindergarten going to be fun?" Molly asked through a mouthful of cereal.

"She asks that every day," Jamie said.

"Hold still, Jamie," Mom said. "Yes, Molly, kindergarten will be lots of fun." She gave Jamie's head a pat. "There."

"What are you going to do today, Mom?" Jamie asked.

"I have a meeting this afternoon at Morgan and Jones, about redesigning their Web site."

"After I go to school?" Molly asked.

"As soon as you get on the after-lunch bus," Mom said. "But I'll be here when you get home."

"I wish I could go to school all day, like Michael and Jamie," Molly said.

"I wish I could go just in the afternoon, like you," Michael said.

A piercing whistle came through the open kitchen window. "Hey, Mike," T.J. called. "Let's go!"

Michael whistled back.

Mom covered her face with her hands and groaned. "Michael, please—not in the house!"

"Sorry." He picked up his backpack and gave her a quick kiss on the cheek.

"Have a good day," she said. "I love you."

"You, too. See you later."

"Come *on*," T.J. said as Michael came out of the garage with his bike. "You know how Brad gets if he thinks he's gonna be late."

Michael grinned. "He always thinks he's going to be late. Don't worry."

"Too bad he's not in the same homeroom with us," T.J. said as they rode down the street.

"He can't help it if his last name begins with a *P*," Michael said. "Anyway, we'll probably be in at least one class together."

Brad was waiting a couple of blocks away. "It's about time," he said as he joined them. "Where've you been?"

"Told you," T.J. said to Michael.

"Chill, Brad," Michael said. "We've got plenty of time."

Lincoln Middle School had been silent all summer, but today it had come back to life. As kids poured out of buses, the boys locked their bikes to the racks. Once in the main door, they pushed their way through the crowd and started up the stairs.

"Hey, Cooper," a dark-haired boy called from the landing above them, "cross-country sign-up this afternoon."

"Right," T.J. called back. "I'll be there."

The hall was swarming with kids, all talking and laughing. As the three boys reached the top of the stairs, the warning bell rang, ten minutes before the late bell. Teachers came out into the hall and began shooing students into their homerooms.

Michael walked into Room 214 and sat down near the back. T.J. took the desk behind him.

Michael knew most of the other kids, since they'd been in the same homeroom last year. But then T.J. poked him between the shoulder blades. "Hey—who's that?"

Michael looked toward the door. A girl he'd never seen before had come in and taken a seat on the other side of the room. She glanced around the room, and when she saw Michael looking at her, she gave him a small smile.

"Do you know her?" T.J. asked.

"No."

The late bell rang, and a man walked into the room. He closed the door and smiled at them. "Good morning," he said. "Welcome back. For any of you who might be new to Lincoln, my name is Mr. Daly. I teach social studies." He picked up a piece of paper from his desk. "I'd like to begin by seating you alphabetically."

He stood in front of the first row and started calling names. "Chapman, Christie—come on, people, let's get this done—Clark, Cleary . . ." When everyone had been rearranged, Michael ended up in the same row, but farther forward. The new girl sat across the aisle, right in front of T.J. Her name was Melanie Cook. She smiled at him again, but he pretended not to notice.

"All right," Mr. Daly said. "Here are emergency cards—get them filled out and bring them back. Here are your class schedules. Please make sure you have your own."

A loud beep came from the PA system. Morning announcements followed, the usual first-day stuff: cafeteria rules, sign-ups for fall sports, information about other activities. Then the principal's voice began: "Welcome back to Lincoln."

As the voice droned on, Michael leaned toward T.J. "He said the same thing last year," he whispered.

"We'll have it memorized by next year," T.J. whispered back.

"Last, but not least," Mr. Daly said when the speaker was silent, "I'm handing out locker combinations. We have ten minutes or so before the bell for first period rings. So go out in the hall and find your locker. Open it, and then come back. Do it *quietly*," he said as they all jumped up. "And please, memorize your combinations."

Michael and T.J. found their lockers and compared schedules. "Looks like we're together for gym, math, and science," Michael said. "Oh, no, we've got Wolf for math."

"My brother had him," T.J. said. "He hated him."

Mr. Daly came out to the hall. "Okay, everyone, back inside." No sooner were they all back in their seats than the bell rang, and they were out the door. School had begun.

In every class, teachers assigned seats and books, and talked about what material they'd be covering. Math, science, social studies, English, foreign language exploration, and an elective. Michael's elective for the first marking period was art, right after lunch.

He'd been glad to get back into the art room. It was where he felt most comfortable. There were no formulas, no equations, just the challenge of seeing something and capturing it on paper. Michael threw himself into his work, often doing a drawing over several times before he felt it was good enough. "Ease up on yourself, Michael," Ms. Simmons had said to him more than once last year. "I don't expect perfection." But at the end of the year he had been the only sixth-grader from Lincoln to have two pieces selected for the all-county middle school art competition. One of them took second place in the drawing category.

Today, Ms. Simmons stood in the doorway, checking names and saying, "Sit anywhere you want." Michael sat at a desk near the front of the room and dug into his backpack, looking for a pencil. When he looked up again, Melanie Cook was sitting at the desk across the aisle from him.

After the bell rang, Ms. Simmons moved to the front of the room. When they were quiet, she said, "Good afternoon, and welcome. I think we're going to have an interesting year."

She walked back and forth across the front of the room, as if she was thinking. Finally, she said, "Rows one and two—turn toward each other and look really carefully at the face of the person across from you until I say 'stop.' Rows three and four, and five and six—do the same."

Michael turned and looked across the aisle, straight into Melanie's eyes. Heat rose up his face to the tops of his ears. He looked at her nose, her eyebrows, her chin, but he kept coming back to those dark blue eyes.

After what seemed like forever, Ms. Simmons said, "Stop." Michael faced forward again. "Now," Ms. Simmons said. "Who can tell me one thing about the face of the person they were looking at? Michael, how about you? No, don't look at her now. Tell me what you saw."

What should he say? That her eyes were the color of the lake where he and Grandpa used to put the boat in? That she had a tiny white scar above her left eyebrow? "Uh—she has little freckles on her nose," he said.

Melanie put her hands over her face. Everyone else laughed.

"All right," Ms. Simmons said, "settle down. That was good, Michael—just the kind of detail I was hoping for. Now, who else?"

When the bell rang, chairs scraped against the floor as everyone stood up. "Hold on," Ms. Simmons said. "There's homework. Nothing major," she added as everyone groaned. "For the next few days, I want you to look at yourselves in the mirror, and look carefully. I'll explain on Friday."

"Freckles?" T.J. said to Michael as they went to their lockers at the end of the day.

Heat flooded Michael's face. "Don't make me sorry I told you that," he said.

"I'll try." T.J. stuffed a couple of books into his backpack. "But jeez, Mike—freckles?"

They met Brad out by the bike rack. They rode together a few blocks, then Michael said, "I'm going to Miller's. See you tomorrow."

Miller's Art Supplies was in a small shopping center a mile or so from the school. Michael locked his bike to a post in front of the store and went inside. A balding man behind the counter smiled. "Michael, hello," he said. "What brings you in?"

"Hi, Mr. Miller. I need some sketching pencils."

Mr. Miller pointed to a box on the counter. "I'm running a special on those six-packs."

"Great."

"Anything else?"

"Not today." Michael paid for the pencils. "Thanks, Mr. Miller. See you later."

As he went outside, he heard laughter. Just beyond Mr. Miller's store was a group of seven or eight older guys, shoving each other, laughing, and talking in loud voices. Some of the language they used made Michael glad Mom wasn't there. Still, that didn't stop him from walking closer to watch the ones with skateboards.

A couple of girls were headed their way from the other direction. They walked faster as they passed the group, one staring straight ahead, the other with her eyes on the ground. One of the guys whistled, long and low, and another one said, "Whoa, baby." The rest laughed and whistled.

What a bunch of jerks. Michael smiled at the girls as they came toward him, but they ignored him, too, and went into a store.

As Michael turned his attention back to the skateboarders, one of them bent down, grabbed the rear bumper of a passing car, and hung on. He rode until the car turned a corner, then he straightened up and rolled a little farther, spun around, and returned to the group. When he stopped, he popped the board up with one foot, caught it, and bowed. The group cheered.

"Hey!" One of the guys had noticed Michael. "What are you looking at?"

"Just watching," Michael said.

"Well, stay out of the way. Unless maybe you want to give it a try?"

Michael didn't take the bait. "No, thanks," he said. Everyone laughed.

"I didn't think so," the boy said. He turned back to his friends. "Yo, Pete, watch it!"

Pete had been trying to balance his board on the back wheels, but it slipped out from under him. He sat down hard on the sidewalk and covered his eyes as his board shot out and rolled under a passing car. Michael held his breath. That board was history. But wait—the car went by and there it was, untouched. The group hooted and shouted. Pete jumped up, whooping louder than any of them. Red-faced, he ran to get his board.

"Hey." The kid who had just told Michael to stay out of the way was standing beside him now. Michael took a step back. "What?"

"If you're gonna stand there, be useful. Hold this for me." He held out his cigarette.

Michael hesitated.

"Come on, I don't have all day."

Michael reached out and took the cigarette, then froze. Another skateboard had gotten away from its owner, and was heading straight for a passing car. It hit the back wheel broadside with a clunk and bounced off. The driver stopped and turned his head. He didn't look at the group for very long before driving away, but it was long enough for Michael to see that it was Mr. Andrews.

He thrust the cigarette back. "I've got to be going."

The other shrugged. "Suit yourself."

All the way home, Michael kept seeing Mr. Andrews's face. *Did he see me? Why did I take that cigarette? What if he says something to Dad?* When he got home, he put his bike in the garage and went inside. "Michael?" Mom called from her office off the kitchen.

"Yeah," Michael called back.

"Where've you been?"

"I went to Miller's for some pencils."

"You know you're supposed to let me know if you're not coming right home."

"Sorry."

"Would you bring in the trash cans?"

"Okay." He headed upstairs to his room and dropped his backpack on his bed.

He didn't see me. He couldn't have. He was busy looking at those other guys. And even if I was hanging out with them, so what?

"Hey." Mom stuck her head in his doorway. "How was your day?"

"Okay."

"Much homework?"

He shook his head.

"Well, after you bring in the cans, why don't you get a snack. Then you can kick back before dinner. It'll just be the four of us. Dad has a meeting."

A while later, Michael wandered into the family room. Jamie and Molly had the television on to some dopey animal program, but they seemed more interested in the castle they were building out of plastic bricks. So he changed the channel.

"Michael!" Jamie shouted. "Put that back."

"No," Michael said. "You're busy with your castle. Anyway, you have to set the table in a few minutes. I want to see this."

"Mama," Molly called, "Michael's being mean."

Mom came into the family room. "What's going on?"

"Michael switched the channel," Jamie said.

"You weren't watching," Michael said.

"Were too."

"Enough." Mom turned the television off. "Dinner's almost ready. Girls, go set the table. Michael," she added as Jamie and Molly left, "remember—you're the oldest. It's up to you to set a good example."

During dinner, Jamie and Molly talked and talked about school. Michael kept his eyes on his plate, only talking when Mom asked him a couple of questions. When dinner was over, the girls cleared the table and he loaded the dishwasher. He tried to watch TV, but he just couldn't concentrate. *Set a good example, Mom said. What would she have thought if she had seen him with that cigarette?*

"Michael," Mom said at last, "are you sure everything's all right?"

"Yeah," he said. "I'm just tired, that's all."

A short time later, he said good night and went upstairs. In his room, he tried to read, but he couldn't turn his mind off. Finally, he closed the book and got ready for bed.

After he washed his face, he looked in the mirror as Ms. Simmons had said to do. "Relax," he said. "He probably didn't see you. But so what if he did? You weren't doing anything wrong."

He went back to his room and got into bed. *Anyway, who cares what he thinks?*

You do. What if he says something to Dad?

He wouldn't. Would he?

He turned out the light and continued to argue with himself until he fell asleep.

Eleven

By the time Friday came, Michael was ready for the weekend.

He could see after only four days that he was going to have real trouble in math. Mr. Wolf had made that plain this morning.

English had run a few minutes overtime, and he hadn't been able to get to his locker for his math homework. In fact, he'd barely made it to math before the bell rang.

Everyone else was already in the room. The Wolfman was still standing in the doorway. As Michael approached, he held out his hand. "Homework?"

"No, sir," Michael said. "I mean, yes, sir."

"Well, which is it? Yes or no?"

"I mean, I did it, but I don't have it with me," Michael said. "Mr. Stewart kept us after the bell, and there wasn't time to get to my locker. And I thought being late would be worse than not having my homework."

Stop babbling. You sound like an idiot. He stopped to catch his breath.

Mr. Wolf stood there with one eyebrow raised. After what seemed like forever, he said, "Okay, Delaney, just this once. But I want that homework before the end of the day. *Before*—after the dismissal bell is no good. Understand?"

"Yes, sir." Michael slipped in and sat down before Wolf could change his mind.

"Now," Mr. Wolf said, "clear your desks and quiet down." He began to pass out papers. "This is just a little test to see what you remember from last year."

Usually Michael thought math class would never end, but today it wasn't nearly long enough. He was still working when the bell rang.

"Come on, Delaney, let's have it." Mr. Wolf's outstretched hand was so close that Michael could have leaned forward and bitten it.

"Now."

Michael seethed. If only he had the nerve to crumple up the paper and throw it in Wolf's face.

He handed over the paper and escaped to the cafeteria.

After lunch, at the beginning of art class, Ms. Simmons said, "For the past few days, I've been letting you draw whatever you want. You've been getting your creative juices flowing again after the summer break." She leaned forward. "Today, though, the work begins."

Everyone laughed.

"So," she said, "today's Friday. How many of you have taken at least one good look in the mirror since Tuesday?"

Everyone raised their hands.

"More than one?"

A few hands stayed up, including Michael's.

Ms. Simmons smiled. "Now—you probably thought we'd start out with line drawing or still life, like last year. But we're not. Instead, we're going to have some fun. We're going to try our hands at portraits."

As she began to talk about facial structure, Michael scribbled notes and little sketches as fast as he could, forgetting everything around him.

Everything, that is, except Melanie Cook.

She had ended up in three of his classes. He glanced across the aisle every now and then. Once she looked at him and smiled. He turned back to his paper and started scribbling harder, his insides feeling as if they were on a trampoline.

At the end of the day, as he stood at his locker getting what he needed for the weekend, he heard someone call, "Hey, Mike!"

It was T.J. "Listen," he said, "Brad and I signed up for cross-country. How about you?"

"I don't think so," Michael said. "You know I hate running. Anyway, I'm going to have my hands full between working for Mr. Andrews and homework. Wolf's already giving me a hard time, and art's going to keep me busy."

"Art who?" T.J.'s grin disappeared when he saw Michael's face. "Hey," he said, "lighten up. It was a joke."

Michael closed his locker. "I was ignoring it," he said, punching T.J. gently on the shoulder. "See you later."

The next day, he arrived at Mr. Andrews's house a little earlier than the week before. This time he knocked on the back door, then went on in. Mr. Andrews was in the kitchen, pouring a cup of coffee.

"Morning," he said, taking a sip and grimacing. "I made it extra strong," he explained. "I just haven't been able to get going the last few days." He took another sip. "You're in luck today," he continued. "It's good weather for outdoor work. Ever plant bulbs?"

"No," Michael said. *Was he going to say anything about that cigarette?*

"There's nothing to it." Mr. Andrews picked up a little onion-shaped thing from the counter. "You dig a small hole. Put this in, this end up, and cover it. Think you can handle that?"

Michael's face reddened. Did he look stupid? Then he saw the twinkle in the man's eyes. "I don't know," he said, picking up a bulb and examining it. "I suppose so."

Mr. Andrews laughed. "Good. The grass needs to be cut first, then there's a bag of these I'd like you to plant."

"Okay."

"One other thing, Michael."

Uh-oh. "What?"

"I saw you the other day with those skateboarders. Please tell me you don't grab the backs of cars."

"I wasn't with them," Michael said. "I was just watching."

Mr. Andrews nodded. "And the cigarette?"

"The guy wanted me to hold it for him. Honest. I don't smoke."

Mr. Andrews looked him right in the eye for a moment. "I believe you," he said.

Michael turned to go outside. Then he turned back. "Mr. Andrews," he said, "are you going to tell my father?"

Mr. Andrews shook his head. "Why should I? I believe what you told me. After all, trust is part of friendship, and I hope we're getting to be friends. As far as I'm concerned, the matter's closed."

Michael thought about this. "Okay," he said. "Thanks. Thanks a lot."

Mr. Andrews had had the mower fixed, and cutting the lawn didn't seem as hard this time. Michael did the backyard first, then the front.

After he put the mower away, he got the brown paper bag of bulbs from the garage. Crocuses and snowdrops, some to go around the base of the big maple tree near the street and more for the bed by the front porch. "I've had them there for years," Mr. Andrews said. "Then, this spring, nothing. Some blasted critter had a good winter's feed on my bulbs."

Michael had just about finished planting by the tree when he heard a bell ring. He looked up and saw Melanie coming across the street on a bright blue bike.

"Hi," she said. She stopped and put one foot on the curb to steady herself.

He sat back on his heels. "Hi. Do you live around here?"

Dumb question.

If Melanie thought it was a dumb question, though,

she didn't show it. She just nodded and said, "Uh-huh. In the blue-and-white house, down there."

"Oh."

That wasn't much better. Jeez.

He picked up the bag of bulbs and fidgeted with it.

"We moved here this summer. My dad got transferred from Boston," she said. "Where do you live?"

"Over on High."

Silence. *Say something, stupid. Just not something stupid.* "So," Michael said at last, "how do you like Lincoln?"

"It's okay," Melanie said. "It's not as big as my last school, but I like that. And I really like my teachers, except for Mr. Wolf."

"Nobody likes him," Michael said.

Melanie pointed to Mr. Andrews's house. "The man who lives here seems nice. If he's outside when I go by, he always says hello."

"Yeah, Mr. Andrews is a pretty good guy," Michael said. "Kind of weird sometimes, but okay."

"Weird how?"

"I don't know. Things he says sometimes. And he watches Saturday morning cartoons."

Melanie laughed. "I think that's cute. Are you related to him?"

Michael shook his head. "No. He's a friend of my dad's, and I've been doing some work for him on Saturdays."

"I know. I saw you out here a couple of weeks ago when I was walking my dog."

Another silence. Finally, Michael got up. "Well, I guess I'd better get back to work."

"Okay. See you in school." Melanie pushed away from the curb and pedaled down the street.

Michael watched her until she turned in at her driveway. Then he tossed the bag of bulbs high in the air. "Yes!" he said, clapping his hands together. He caught the bag in one hand and continued to toss it as he went whistling up the sidewalk.

When he'd planted the bulbs by the porch, Michael walked around to the back door, went inside, and washed his hands at the kitchen sink. He found Mr. Andrews in the studio, standing by the window, just staring out. When he heard Michael, he turned around. "All done?" he asked.

"All done."

"Good. Now, let's see what you remember from last week." Mr. Andrews pulled a chair over to the window. "Sit."

Michael sat.

Mr. Andrews handed him a sketch pad and pencil. "Draw that corner of the garage, and the trees and fence behind it. Remember what I said about control."

Michael drew. *Relax here. Tighten here. Use the whole arm now.* When he was satisfied with what he'd done, he said, "I'm finished."

"Let's see." Mr. Andrews took the sketch pad. "Good. Very good. I like that bit right here. If you did it again, though, you might want to shade a little more, there."

He gave the sketch pad back to Michael. "That's enough for today."

Michael stood up and stretched.

"I'm glad one of us has accomplished something," Mr. Andrews said. "I seem to be suffering from inertia."

"What's that?"

"You'll get to it in science sometime. A body at rest tends to want to stay that way." He sighed. "Who knows—maybe it's just the change of season."

He raised his eyebrows and held his hand near his mouth, waggling his fingers. "And that's the most ridiculous thing I ever hoid," he said with a grin.

"What?"

"Oh, come on," Mr. Andrews said. "Groucho Marx. You've heard of the Marx Brothers, haven't you?"

"I'm not sure. Were they a singing group?"

Mr. Andrews shook his head. "Oh, Lord, what's this world coming to? You mean you've never seen a Marx Brothers movie?"

"No."

"Well, my boy, that's about to change. Come on."

Michael followed him down to the living room. "What's the name of this movie?" he asked as he sat on the couch.

"*Animal Crackers*," Mr. Andrews said as he turned on the television. "Made in 1930." When he looked at Michael he laughed. "Relax," he said, putting a disc into the DVD player. "It's an old movie, made when humor was funny stuff, not four-letter words strung together. Just watch."

The scene, in black-and-white, was an elegant party. Suddenly there appeared a little man with glasses, a large mustache, and bushy eyebrows. He was smoking a huge cigar. Michael leaned forward and listened as the man began to sing:

"Hello, I must be going.
I cannot stay, I came to say I must be going.
I'm glad I came, but just the same, I must be going."

"Hey," Michael said, "I've seen that guy in cartoons."

"*That's* Groucho Marx," Mr. Andrews said, "and he was a person before he was a cartoon. Now, hush."

Michael hushed and watched. When the movie was over, he stood up and stretched. "That was pretty funny," he said, "but there was some stuff I didn't get."

"Don't worry about it," Mr. Andrews said. "It's supposed to be like that. I've seen it a dozen times, and there's some stuff I still don't get. But it always makes me laugh. Now, how about a glass of cider?"

In the kitchen, Michael got two glasses from a cupboard, and Mr. Andrews filled them. They went back to the living room and sat down. Michael looked around at the pictures on the walls. "Mr. Andrews," he said, "how do you decide what to paint?"

"Interesting question." Mr. Andrews frowned. "Sometimes, something just feels right—you know?"

Michael nodded.

"Other times, I get an idea, and I think there's something there, but I'm not quite sure. So I think about it.

And I think some more. After a while, I look at that piece of expensive white paper or canvas and ask myself, 'Charlie, do you want to spoil that?' And I go back to thinking. Finally I get tired of thinking and start painting."

Michael thought of all the paper he'd thrown out because of false starts. Maybe Mr. Andrews was onto something.

"Anything else?" Mr. Andrews asked.

"I can't think of anything right now," Michael said. "But I was wondering if you had a book on drawing faces that I could borrow. We're doing portraits at school, and—"

"Say no more. I have one I think you'd like. However, I have a couple of conditions."

Michael looked at him suspiciously.

"First, you'll have to go up and get it. It should be on the second shelf, somewhere on the left, with a bright blue cover."

"Okay."

"Second, I'd like you to start calling me Charlie."

Michael raised an eyebrow. "Charlie?"

"That's what all my friends call me. And we're getting to be friends. At least I hope we are."

"Well . . . okay." *Charlie. Hi, Charlie. How are you, Charlie?* This was going to take some getting used to.

"How about you?" the man said. "Do your friends call you Michael? Mike? You know, when I was your age, I had a friend named Michael, and we called him Mickey."

"No," Michael said. "I mean, Michael's fine."

Mr. Andrews leaned forward, concern showing in his blue eyes. "Is Mickey what your grandfather called you?"

Michael nodded.

"I'm sorry."

Michael shrugged. "That's okay. You didn't know."

Mr. Andrews sat back. "Michael it is, then."

Michael went up to the studio. It took him a few minutes to find the book. When he came down, he paused at the living room door. Mr. Andrews was stretched out on the couch, his eyes closed.

"See you next week, Charlie," Michael said softly. There was no answer, just a little snore. Michael went to the kitchen, put the book in his backpack, and left, closing the door quietly behind him.

Twelve

"I'm never going to survive math," Michael said as he set his lunch on the cafeteria table and slid into a chair next to Brad the following Friday.

"Hey," T.J. said from across the table, "I'm trying to eat here."

"Go ahead, laugh." Michael took a bite of his sandwich. "You're doing fine in there. I spend more time studying for that class than all my others put together. And that's where I'm doing the worst."

"You know, I read one time about a guy who taught a course called Mind over Math," Brad said. "Maybe that's what you need. Maybe you're one of those—whaddaya call 'em?—math phobics."

"You're a lot of help," Michael said. "You guys are always the first ones done with the Friday tests. And by the way—do you see *me* sitting on the smart side of the room?"

"Aw, come on," T.J. said. "You don't believe that, do you?"

Michael jammed a straw into a container of milk and

took a long swig. "Everyone knows Wolf has the room divided into smart and dumb. And everyone knows which side is which."

"Listen, Mike," Brad said. "Maybe you just have to try a little harder. You going to eat that cookie?"

Michael shoved the cookie toward Brad. "Try *harder*?"

Everyone nearby turned to look at him.

Michael lowered his voice. "I'm trying as hard as I can. But just when I think I get what's going on, the rules change and I'm right back where I started."

He stuffed the empty milk container into his lunch bag and wadded it up. "And because I didn't get the stuff we did first, I don't get what we're doing now."

"Have you talked to Wolf?" Brad asked.

"Yeah. Tuesday, during lunch, after I got all of Monday's homework wrong. He started off by telling me that when he saw my name on his class list, he figured I'd do really well—'since your father's such a good teacher,' he said. He showed me what I did wrong on the homework, then told me to try the first few problems again. So I did, while he sat there, watching. And I felt pretty good, because I got different answers. Unfortunately, they still weren't the right ones."

He rocked his chair back. "Lunch period was just about over by then. That's when he said that for anyone else he'd probably suggest finding a tutor, but in my case I could just ask my dad."

"That's not a bad idea," T.J. said. "If my dad was a math teacher, I'd ask him for help."

"It's kind of hard to ask when I hardly ever see him."

T.J. stood up. "I gotta tell you, Mike," he said, "you really know how to give a meal atmosphere." He looked at his watch. "I have to go talk to Coach about the meet this afternoon."

"I'll come with you," Brad said. "See you later, Mike."

Michael watched them cross the cafeteria and start talking with a teacher standing near the door. What just happened? They were supposed to be his friends, and they just walked away.

The bell rang. He threw his lunch bag in the trash and went up the stairs to Ms. Simmons's room.

Melanie was already there, in her seat across the aisle from his. She was searching for something, taking things out of her backpack and digging around inside. At last, she stuffed everything back in and shoved the backpack under her chair. "I can't believe I don't have a pencil," she said to Michael. "Do you have an extra one?"

Michael reached into his backpack and pulled out a pencil. "Here," he said, handing it to Melanie.

"Thanks," she said. "You're a lifesaver."

She had an amazing smile. Michael had never seen anyone with teeth as white as hers. They could have been in a toothpaste ad.

The bell rang, and Ms. Simmons called the class to order.

She had started last week by talking about portraits, telling them about facial structure and feature placement. She'd even shown them pictures of what was under the skin—bones and muscles.

"That's gross," Erin Smith said.

"Especially after lunch," Kristi Norton added.

Ms. Simmons just smiled and said, "Art is more than picking up a pencil and making a pretty picture. You need to understand what's beneath the surface."

Just like fishing. What had Grandpa said? *You don't just drop a line in any old place, Mickey. You have to be familiar with the water, and know what's under the surface.*

Then Ms. Simmons had shown them slides of portraits by famous artists. She told them what was special about each one, and about the artists themselves, what influenced them, and why they painted the way they did.

Finally, she let them start drawing. They started with small sketches of each other, practicing getting things in the right places. She had them form groups so that each of them was looking at the side of someone else's face. Michael positioned himself so he could draw Melanie. With each sketch he got a little better, managing to get the shape of her nose just right, and the way she bit her lower lip when she was concentrating.

As they worked today, Ms. Simmons walked around, stopping to look and comment. "Don't worry about getting a photographic likeness," she said. "Right now, just get the eyes and nose where they're supposed to be."

She stopped by Michael's desk and looked over his shoulder. "Good, Michael," she said. "Watch the jawline, here. Why don't you try a three-quarters profile," she added. "And would you see me on your way out? I have something I think you might find interesting." She went on to the next desk, leaving behind a trace of the spicy perfume that always made him think of her as Ms. Cinnamon.

As he worked, everything else slipped away. Ms. Simmons's voice brought him back. "I'm sure you know by now that portraits aren't easy," she said. "But you're all coming along. I'm seeing some really nice work.

"Now," she continued, "even though we'll be on this unit for a few weeks yet, I want to talk about your final projects so you'll have plenty of time. The bell's going to ring in a minute, so listen. What I want you to do is choose a photograph of a person—any photograph, whether it's someone you know or a picture from a magazine. It can be any view—side, three-quarters, or full on." The bell rang. "Hold it," she said as they all stood up. "From that photograph, you're going to do a really polished piece of work. Take your time. Study that face. Really get to know it. Do sketches first, and save them. What you'll hand in is a packet showing the development of a portrait, from rough start to finished product." She opened the door. "Okay—now you can go."

When everyone else had gone, Michael stopped at Ms. Simmons's desk. "You wanted to see me?" he asked.

"Yes." She rummaged through a pile of papers on her desk. "There's a flyer here somewhere. Aha." She handed him a bright yellow sheet of paper. "Take a look at this while I write you a late pass."

Annual Arts Competition, the flyer said. *This year's theme is* We Each Need a Hero. *Theme may be portrayed in writ-*

ing, music, or visual arts. "You think I should enter this?" he said.

"It's up to you," Ms. Simmons said. "But I think you'd have a good chance. Perhaps you could tie it in with your class project. It's a while before the deadline. Think about it."

A couple of hours later, the last bell of the day rang, and Michael was free until Monday. Outside, as he unlocked his bike, he watched the cross-country team heading for their bus. Brad and T.J. didn't see him.

He could hear voices singing "Happy Birthday." A group of girls was serenading Melanie, who was trying to make them stop. By the time the song was over, Melanie was laughing so hard that she didn't pay attention to where she was going and walked right into one of the small trees that lined the walk. This only made them laugh more. Michael grinned. Who'd have thought she was a klutz?

He didn't think she'd seen him. But just before she boarded one of the bright yellow buses, she turned and waved at him.

He waved back, even though he wasn't sure where she was sitting. Then he got on his bike and rode home.

When he got there, Mom's office door was closed. "I'm home," he called.

"Hi," Mom called back. "Let me finish what I'm doing, then I'll come talk."

"Okay." He poured a glass of milk, helped himself to a couple of cookies, and went up to his room.

He took the flyer about the arts competition out of his backpack and read it again. *We Each Need a Hero.* What was a hero, exactly? He got out his dictionary and opened it to the *h*'s. *Heritage. Hermit.* Here it was: *Hero: One admired for bravery, great deeds or noble qualities, a role model or ideal.*

He looked over at the photo of him and Grandpa. Grandpa had gotten a medal when he was a soldier. So he must have been brave, or done something great. Michael had sure looked up to him and wanted to be like him. Wasn't that what they meant by a role model?

He picked up a pencil and began to doodle. No details, just the outline of the figures. Then he picked up the photo and looked at it more closely, searching for the sort of things he could use to bring a drawing to life. Tears began to well up in back of his eyes, and he put the photo down. No. He wouldn't cry.

He started to crumple up the paper. But he stopped, smoothed out the wrinkles as well as he could, and put it into his art folder. As he did, one of the sketches he'd done of Melanie fell out and dropped to the floor. He picked it up and tacked it onto his bulletin board.

What could he do to get her to smile that toothpaste ad smile at him again?

A birthday card. That was it. He'd make her a birthday card, and stop by her house with it when he was finished at Charlie's tomorrow. After all, it was just down the street.

Maybe he should call her, to be sure she'd be there.

No. He didn't want her to think he was planning anything. This had to look spontaneous.

Maybe he'd just look up her number, in case he ever needed it. He found the phone book in the kitchen. As he stood fumbling through it, the phone rang beside him, making him jump.

"Hello, Michael." It was Charlie. "Listen, I'm not feeling too good. I must have picked up a bug earlier in the week. You'd better not come tomorrow. I don't think it's anything catching, but it's best not to take a chance. Next week for sure, all right?"

"Yeah. Charlie?"

"Yes?"

"You're sure you don't want me to do anything?"

"I'm sure, Michael. Thanks for asking, though."

"Okay. I hope you feel better."

All right. He had the whole day off tomorrow. He could still go by Melanie's in the morning. And he'd call T.J. and Brad, and they could do something together. It would be the way Saturdays used to be.

So why wasn't he happier?

Thirteen

"There. Finished."

Michael pushed the chair back from his desk and looked long and hard at the drawing in front of him. He'd gotten up early to put the finishing touches on the card he'd made for Melanie last night. The colors in the bunch of autumn flowers he'd drawn—purples, golds, greens—glowed against the rough gray paper.

What to write inside? Nothing too funny. Nothing mushy. Maybe just "Happy Birthday." The picture was the important thing, anyway.

He needed an envelope. He took another piece of paper, folded and glued it, put the card inside, and taped it shut. Then, with his calligraphy pen, the one with the wide nib, he wrote "Melanie" on the front in his best italic writing.

Perfect.

As he went down for breakfast, he could hear Mom and Dad in the kitchen. Good. He could ask Dad for help with math. He'd be getting A's and B's in no time, and the Wolfman would finally get off his case.

But at the bottom of the stairs, he stopped. "I don't know," he heard Dad say. "Right now, I'm beginning to regret ever starting this Ph.D."

"Why?" Mom asked.

"I am so close to finishing that last section of the dissertation," Dad said. "Now that school's started, it's been hard to find the time to work on it. And when I do, part of my mind is on lesson plans for the next day." He sighed. "It's all just starting to get to me."

"You've come this far," Mom said. "It'd be a shame to give up now."

There was a silence. She was probably rubbing Dad's shoulders the way she always did when he was bothered about something.

"Take the whole day and go work at the library," she said. "Just get away from all the distractions around here."

"You're sure?" Dad said.

"Mmmhmm. Now, go. Write. Finish."

"Okay," Dad said. A chair scraped on the kitchen floor. "I'll see you later."

Michael waited until he heard the back door close. Then he counted slowly to ten and walked into the kitchen.

"Morning," Mom said. "You just missed Dad. He won't be back until dinnertime." She stood up and put her coffee mug into the sink. "You're up earlier than I expected. I thought you had the day off."

"I do. But I have an errand to run this morning."

"An errand?"

"I just have to take something over to someone's house. Someone from school."

He quickly ate a bowl of cereal and washed it down with a glass of orange juice. Then he went to the phone and dialed T.J.'s number. All he got was the answering machine. The Coopers had changed their message again. They always had funny, weird ones. This time it was the whole family singing, *"We're the Coopers / We're not home / Leave your name and number / at the tone"* to the tune of "Frère Jacques." After the beep, Michael said, "Hey, T.J., it's me. I've got the day off. I have to do something this morning, but then I'll be home. Think of something to do and call me."

He brushed his teeth, then grabbed the card from his desk. "Back later," he called to Mom as he went out the door.

It was a quiet morning, and he saw only a few people as he rode to Melanie's house. He slowed down as he passed Charlie's. The morning paper was still in the driveway. Charlie must be sleeping late.

Michael stopped his bike in Melanie's driveway and checked his watch. Ten o'clock. He hoped she was up. And dressed. At the thought of catching her in her pajamas, his face went hot. He waited until it cooled down, then leaned his bike against the garage and started toward the front door.

He'd only taken a couple of steps when the door flew open and out charged the biggest, shaggiest gray dog he'd ever seen, pulling Melanie behind him. She had a tight grip on her end of the leash and was shouting, "Grover, you jerk, slow down!"

When Grover saw Michael, he stopped and stood still. Melanie didn't stop fast enough and tripped over the dog, landing on the grass beside him. "Grover," she said, "what's with you?"

Then she saw Michael.

"Hi," she said as she picked herself up. "Why aren't you at Mr. Andrews's house?"

"Got the day off," Michael said. He eyed Grover, who grinned at him, showing a mouthful of large white teeth. "What kind of dog is he?"

"Just a mutt," Melanie said. "My dad says he's probably seven or eight different kinds, and the worst part of each."

"Is he friendly?"

"He's a cream puff. I'll show you—come here."

Michael took a few steps forward.

"Hold out your hand."

Keeping the card in his left hand, behind his back, Michael reached his right hand toward Grover, palm down. Grover sniffed at it, wagged his tail, then sat down and offered a paw.

"Hey, that's great." Michael shook the dog's paw. "Did you teach him that?"

"He started doing it on his own when he was a pup." Melanie scratched Grover's head. "We just kind of encouraged it."

Grover stood up, stretched, and looked back at Melanie and Michael.

"Okay, we're coming," Melanie said. "We were just going for a walk," she said to Michael. "Come on."

They walked down the driveway, stopping now and then when Grover wanted to check something out. Suddenly Melanie said, "If you don't have to work today, how come you're over this way?"

Michael held out the envelope. "Here."

Melanie took the envelope and opened it. When she saw the card, her eyes got big. "Oh, wow," she said. "This is beautiful. Thank you."

There was that smile.

"You're so good in art," Melanie said as they walked along the curb. "I wish I could draw as well as you."

"Your stuff's good," Michael said.

"Not like yours. How do you do it?"

"I don't know. It just sort of comes. How do you do so well in math?"

Melanie thought for a moment. "Same thing, I guess," she said at last.

"You're lucky," Michael said. "Wolf leaves you alone."

"Yeah." Melanie nodded. "What's his problem with you, anyway?"

Michael shrugged his shoulders. "I guess he thinks I should be acing his class because my dad's a math teacher at the high school."

"So—my mom's a nurse but the sight of blood makes me sick."

"Does anybody expect you to set a broken bone or stitch up a cut?"

"No."

"It's not quite the same thing, then."

Melanie nodded. "I guess not. Have you asked your dad for help?"

"Uh-uh. He's really busy—besides teaching, he's been writing a Ph.D. dissertation. He wants to teach college math." He kicked at a stone. "I heard him talking with Mom this morning. From the way he sounded, I don't think I should dump anything more on him."

As they walked back up Melanie's driveway, neither one said anything. At the garage, Michael picked up his bike. "I'd better get going."

"Okay." Melanie pulled Grover out of the way. "See you Monday."

"Yeah."

Michael rode down the driveway, stopping to wait for a car to go by. He looked back at Melanie, who waved the card. "Thanks again," she called. He waved back and started for home. As he went by Charlie's house, he noticed that the paper was still in the driveway.

Charlie never slept this late. He must have forgotten to come out for it.

He laid his bike on the driveway, picked up the paper, and ran to the front porch, setting the paper by the door. He chuckled as he imagined Charlie trying to figure out how it got there.

It was a little past eleven when he got home. "Hi," Mom said as she came into the kitchen on her way to the basement with a basket of laundry. "Did you get your errand done?"

"Uh-huh. Did T.J. call?"

"The phone hasn't rung all morning."

Michael went to the phone and called T.J. After a couple of rings, T.J.'s mother answered.

"Hi, Mrs. Cooper. It's Michael. Can I talk to T.J.?"

"He's not here, Michael. He and Brad and some of the other boys from the cross-country squad already had plans. Can I have him call you when he gets home?"

"Sure, Mrs. Cooper. Thanks."

Up in his room, Mom had left some clean clothes on his bed for him to put away. On top of the pile was his Three Musketeers shirt. It had a big picture of a candy bar on the front, and his name on the back. He and T.J. and Brad had each sent away for one after they'd seen the movie. They'd started calling each other by Musketeer names—he was Athos, Brad was Porthos, and T.J. was Aramis—and they'd gone around all that summer pretending to have duels and shouting, "All for one and one for all!"

He should have called T.J. yesterday. But T.J. had been at the cross-country meet. He and Brad probably made those plans with the guys from the team before they got home. They didn't include Michael because they assumed he'd be busy, the way he'd been every Saturday morning since he'd started working for Charlie.

But they were his best friends. Weren't they?

He picked up the shirt. All for one and one for all? Maybe, but it didn't feel like it right now. He opened the closet door and tossed the shirt onto the top shelf.

A couple of years ago, he'd had a fight with T.J. just before leaving for the farm. He couldn't remember now what it had been about, but it had seemed important at the time. He'd told Grandpa all about it, and said he and T.J. weren't friends anymore.

Grandpa had just smiled. *Yes, you are.*

No, we aren't.

Listen, Mickey—a man needs his friends, just like crops need rain. Good friends are hard to find, so when one comes along, you want to tend that friendship, keep it healthy. It might change some as you change, but that's all right. The important thing is to keep the friendship going.

Does that mean never fighting?

Heck, no. Go ahead, argue with him, give him space when he needs it. Just don't push him out.

Grandpa had been right then. By the time Michael and T.J. saw each other again, the fight had been forgotten.

But this was different. Was this what Grandpa had meant by change? If so, Michael didn't like it. "Why can't things stay the same?" he asked the photo on the nightstand. "Everything's changing so fast."

Grandpa's face just smiled back at him. Michael could almost hear him say, *Hang in there, Mickey. Things will work out fine.*

With a sigh, Michael reached up and took the shirt off the closet shelf and put it at the bottom of the pile in his dresser drawer. He'd keep the shirt. But it might be a while before he wore it again.

“Good morning, people. I hope you had a pleasant weekend,” Mr. Wolf said. “On the whole, Friday’s tests were pretty good.”

The class breathed a collective sigh of relief.

“Of course, there *are* some who aren’t living up to their potential,” he continued, looking right at Michael. “They know who they are, and I hope they’ll do better next time.” He gave them one of the toothy smiles that had helped give him the name Wolfman, and began to return their tests.

This was the worst thing about Mondays. Mr. Wolf walked up and down the aisles, handing everybody their papers. He always started on the far side of the room, the smart side. Today was no different.

Brad sat in the first row. “Excellent, as usual, Mr. Parker,” Mr. Wolf said. No surprise—Brad was always top in the class. A few seats later, “Nice work, Miss Cook.” Melanie smiled. Just a couple of rows away, now. “Cooper, this is what I like to see.” T.J. blew out a sigh of relief.

At last, Mr. Wolf stopped at Michael's desk. He gave Michael his paper and looked down at him.

Michael looked at his score. Sixty-seven. His mouth went dry.

"What's going on, Delaney?" Mr. Wolf asked.

"I don't know," Michael said. It was like talking with a mouthful of cotton.

"Did you take my suggestion?"

"No."

Mr. Wolf tapped his finger on Michael's desk. "Maybe *I* should talk to your father. What do you think?"

A talk with the Wolfman. That's all Dad needed. "Look," Michael said, "just leave him out of this. And get off my back."

The rest of the class sat motionless as Mr. Wolf stared into Michael's eyes. Michael returned the stare. Each refused to back down.

"That's it," Mr. Wolf said at last. "I've had enough of your attitude. Take your things and go to the office. *Now.*"

Michael packed up his books in silence, not daring to look at anyone. As he opened the door, Mr. Wolf said, "Oh—Delaney?"

Michael turned around. As he did, he saw Melanie. She looked as if she was going to cry.

"Make sure you get there," Mr. Wolf said. "They'll be expecting you."

Michael took the long way, going across to the other side of the building, down the far stairs, then back toward the office. He walked in and stood at the counter.

Mrs. Young, the office secretary, smiled at him. "Hello, Michael. Can I help you?"

"Mr. Wolf sent me," Michael said, without raising his eyes. "I guess I'm supposed to see Mr. McCormick."

"Let me check," she said. "Have a seat for a minute." She picked up her phone and said a few quiet words, then went back to her work.

Michael sat down on a chair in the corner of the waiting area and picked at a crack in the black vinyl seat. He just wanted to get this over with. What would it be? Endless detention? Suspension? How was he going to explain this at home?

"Michael?"

Wait a minute. This wasn't the principal. This was Mr. Hutchins, his guidance counselor. "I haven't seen you for a while," he said. "Why don't we sit down and talk a bit?"

They went into his office. Michael sat in a chair next to the battered green metal desk.

Mr. Hutchins sat in his big black chair and leaned back. "Having some trouble in math?"

Michael's shoulders sagged. "Mr. Wolf acts like he hates me. He says I'm not trying. I am, but I don't understand it. When I think I do, it turns out I don't."

"Why did he send you here today?"

"Didn't he already tell you?"

"I'd like to hear it from you."

Michael stared at his knees. "He said he was going to talk to Dad. I blew up at him." He looked at Mr.

Hutchins. "I know I shouldn't have done that. But he wasn't being fair. Just because Dad's a math teacher doesn't mean math is going to be easy for me, does it?"

Mr. Hutchins shook his head.

"On Fridays, Wolfman—I mean, Mr. Wolf—gives us a test. On Mondays, he hands the tests back. Every week my grade gets worse. I feel so stupid. It's just not fair."

Mr. Hutchins shook his head again and sat up straight. "Michael, you're not stupid," he said. "And you're right—math ability isn't genetic." He took off his glasses and rubbed his eyes. "Unfortunately, Michael, I can't make Mr. Wolf change his methods. That, I'm afraid, you'll have to live with. I'll talk to him, though. Maybe I can get him to ease up on you a little." He put his glasses back on. "Meanwhile, you need to think of some way to do better in there. Any ideas?"

Michael shook his head.

"Have you asked him for help?"

"Once. It didn't go very well. I haven't asked him since."

"Why not?"

Michael thought a moment. "I guess I just don't want to be around him any more than I have to. Anyway, I told you he doesn't like me. He probably wouldn't help me even if I did ask."

"Oh, I think he would," Mr. Hutchins said. "But it's your choice." He stood up and walked over to the window. Turning back to Michael, he said, "So, let's think about this. Do you do much cooking at home?"

"No." What did cooking have to do with this?

"Okay. What if I put you in a kitchen, gave you a recipe, and told you to prepare it. What would you do?"

Michael thought. "Read the recipe first, I guess."

"Good. And what if there were some terms you didn't understand in that recipe? What then?"

"I'd ask you to explain them."

"And if I didn't? Or wouldn't?"

"I'd ask someone else."

Mr. Hutchins smiled.

"You mean I should ask someone else?" Michael said.

Mr. Hutchins nodded.

"Like Dad?"

Mr. Hutchins sat down again. "He seems like the obvious choice."

"I know," Michael said, "but this isn't a good time."

"What do you mean?"

"He's been writing his Ph.D. dissertation, and it's got him really stressed. Anyway, I hardly ever see him. I never know when he's going to be home, so how can I count on him for help?"

"Make an appointment."

Michael frowned. "An appointment? Like with a doctor?"

"Sure. Why not? Michael, I can't believe he wouldn't find time for you if he knew you needed help."

Michael shifted in his chair, thinking. At last, he looked at Mr. Hutchins. "I don't know—maybe."

Mr. Hutchins smiled. "If not him, then someone else. But you'd better ask someone. Okay?"

"Okay."

The bell rang. As if on cue, Michael's stomach growled.

Mr. Hutchins laughed. "Lunchtime?"

Michael nodded.

Mr. Hutchins waved him toward the door. "Go on. And if you need anything, come see me."

Michael walked into the cafeteria and sat down with Brad, T.J., and some others from the cross-country team.

"Whoa, here's the guy with the death wish," Brad said.

"Yeah, Mike, thanks," T.J. said. "After you left, Wolf was a pain in the butt for the rest of the period."

"Cut it out." Michael fished in his backpack for his lunch.

"You better watch out," T.J. continued, enjoying himself. "The Wolfman is out for blood now." He gave a howl. The others at the table laughed and howled, too.

Michael pushed his chair back. "You think you're so funny. But you know what? You're not."

He picked up his things and moved to a nearby empty table.

Brad followed him. "Mike, wait. We didn't mean anything, honest. Come on."

Michael shook his head.

"Fine," Brad said. "Have it your way." He started back to his table, then stopped and turned around. "Hey, Mike," he said. "Still friends?"

"Sure," Michael said. "Why not?"

"I don't know. You're just acting kind of weird, that's all."

"I'm okay, Brad. Really. Don't worry."

Brad didn't look too sure about that. "All right," he said. "Catch you later."

As Michael sat picking at his sandwich, there was a tap on his shoulder. He looked up and saw Melanie.

"Hey," he said.

"How are you?" she asked.

"Fine. Why wouldn't I be?"

"Wolf really came down hard on you."

Michael shrugged.

"Don't let him get to you," she said. "It's not worth it."

"That's easy for you to say," Michael said.

Melanie hesitated. Then she said, "Look, I'm not a math genius. But I do understand what's going on in there. Want some help?"

"You mean it?"

"Sure."

"When?"

"I don't know. Homeroom period? Maybe we could get library passes."

A whistle came from Brad and T.J.'s table. "Hey, Mike," T.J. called, "I can see why you didn't want to sit with us."

"Aw, T.J." Before Michael could say anything else, the bell rang. Laughing, T.J. and the others escaped into the hall.

Michael turned back to Melanie. Should he ask her if

she wanted to walk to art together? But she was already halfway to the door with a couple of other girls Michael didn't know. Both disappointed and relieved, he picked up his backpack and headed off to class.

Later, as Michael was getting his books from his locker, he heard another locker bang shut and saw T.J. coming over.

"Hey, Mike, what's going on?"

Michael bent over to pick up a pen from the bottom of his locker. "What do you mean?"

"Come on, Mike, this is me. You've been real touchy lately."

Michael straightened up and looked at T.J. "You can't think of one reason?"

"You knew we were kidding at lunch."

Michael closed his locker. "Look, I just have a lot on my mind right now."

"Like what?"

"Like math."

"What else?"

"I've been thinking a lot about the arts contest. Ms. Simmons thinks I should enter."

"That hero thing? What are you going to do?"

"A portrait of Grandpa, I think."

T.J. leaned against the lockers. "You miss him a lot, don't you?"

Michael bit his lip. "Yeah."

"Look, Mike—" T.J. began, but a whistle from down the hall interrupted him.

"Hey, Cooper, you know how Coach gets if you're late."

Michael picked up his backpack. "You'd better get going. And listen—I'm going to start taking the bus tomorrow. I have to bring some stuff for art that I don't want to try and carry on my bike. So don't stop for me."

"Mike—"

"Cooper, come on!"

"Okay!" T.J. shouted back. "Well," he said to Michael, "see you tomorrow."

"Right." Michael watched as T.J. loped down the hall. Then, slinging his backpack over his shoulder, he headed off in the other direction.

Fifteen

A couple of days later, when Michael walked into art class, Ms. Simmons stopped him. “Have you decided about the arts contest?” she asked.

“Yes,” he said. “I’m going to enter. And I’m going to use the portrait I do for the final project.”

“Great.” Ms. Simmons smiled. “Have you started yet?”

“Uh-huh. I’ve been doing a lot of sketches at home.”

“I can’t wait to see what you end up with.”

After school, Michael and T.J. walked out the door into the bright September sunshine. “Come on, Mike,” T.J. said. “It’s only Wednesday. You put in your time for this guy on Saturdays. Can’t you get the book then?”

Michael stopped beside his bus. “No.”

“But this is the first time practice has been canceled. I thought you and Brad and I could go shoot some baskets or something.”

“That’s what I thought last Saturday.”

“Hey, hold on,” T.J. said. “How were we supposed to know you’d have the day off?”

“So, this is the same thing.”

They stared at each other for a moment. Then Michael looked away. It wasn't that he couldn't wait. He just didn't want to.

"Fine. Forget it." T.J. walked off without another word.

Michael watched him go, then stepped up and into the bus. Melanie was sitting toward the rear, alone. In what he hoped was a casual manner, he walked back and said, "Hi."

Melanie looked up from the book in her lap. "Oh, hi."

"I was wondering if you want to study tomorrow for Friday's math test."

"Sure."

He looked at her backpack on the seat beside her. "Are you saving this?"

"No." She moved the backpack. "You can sit there."

Michael sat. Neither of them spoke. Melanie looked out the window, and Michael studied a worn spot in the knee of his jeans. In a few minutes, the bus was full. It started up with a jerk, and he bumped against her shoulder. It happened again a moment later, when the bus hit a pothole in the driveway. His face burned as he tried to balance his backpack on his knees with one hand and brace himself on the seat with the other.

But then, as the bus turned onto the street, she leaned against him, just slightly. He stared straight ahead, but managed to catch a glimpse of her out of the corner of his eye. Her cheeks were pink, and there was a little smile at the corners of her mouth.

He cleared his throat. "So, do you know who you're going to draw for your final portrait project?"

"Not really. I'll probably use a magazine picture instead of someone I know. That way, if it doesn't turn out very well, nobody will get mad. How about you?"

"My grandfather."

"I bet he'll like that."

"He's dead."

"Oh." She bit her lip. "I'm sorry. I didn't know."

"That's okay. How would you? He had a heart attack this summer." That was the first time he'd said it out loud.

They lapsed back into silence as the bus jolted along. When it stopped at the corner of High and Longview, Michael made no move to get up. Melanie nudged him. "Isn't this your stop?"

"Not today. I'm going by Charlie's to see if I can borrow a book, so I'm getting off at your stop."

A few minutes later, the bus stopped at the corner of Longview and Maple. The only ones to get off were Melanie and Michael. He could hear giggles and whispers as they stood up and walked to the front. Tongues would be flapping tomorrow.

As they walked from the corner toward Melanie's house, Michael looked across the street. A few houses down, Charlie was by the curb, getting his trash cans. He picked up a can and started up the driveway, but after only a few steps he stopped and put it down.

Michael looked at Melanie. "I've got to go," he said.

"See you tomorrow." Sprinting across the street, he called, "Hey, Charlie—wait a minute."

Charlie straightened up and turned around. When he saw Michael, he broke into a wide smile. "Hello," he said. "What brings you over here in the middle of the week?"

Michael caught his breath, then took a trash can in each hand. "I was hoping I could borrow another book," he said as they walked up the driveway. "I noticed another one about portraits the last time." He set the cans down inside the open garage door. "Say, Charlie, are you okay?"

"Don't you worry about me," Charlie said. "I'm fine—just a little tired." He winked. "Too many late nights out with the girls, you know."

Michael snorted. "Right."

"Guess I'll have to behave for a while, though," Charlie said. "Jean's coming in for a visit."

"When?"

"Tomorrow. She's looking forward to meeting you."

"Oh. Okay." *What had Charlie told her about him?*

Charlie grinned. "Go on up and get your book. You know where they are."

Michael left his backpack and jacket on the kitchen table and went upstairs. When he came back down, Charlie was pouring milk into a mug of coffee. "Find what you were looking for?" he asked.

Michael showed him the book.

"That's a good one," Charlie said. "Now, can you stay for a while?"

“I guess so,” Michael said. “But I’d better call home and tell Mom. She gets mad if I don’t let her know I’m going to be late.”

“I understand. I’ll be in the living room.”

After Michael hung up the phone, he took the glass of milk Charlie had left for him on the table and went into the living room. Charlie was standing by the TV with a DVD in his hand.

“I found this at that rental place near the mall,” he said. “I was going to show it to you on Saturday, but why wait?”

He slipped the disc into the DVD player. “Ever hear of Norman Rockwell?”

“Is he the guy who did a picture of himself doing a self-portrait?” Michael asked.

“That’s the one.”

“Okay. Ms. Simmons showed us some of his stuff.”

“Good for her. Rockwell spent most of his life painting people’s faces, Michael. You can learn a lot by studying his work.” He pushed a button and the DVD began to play.

Michael drank it all in. An old woman, her gnarled hands clasped in prayer. The happy faces of a family gathered around a Thanksgiving table. A young girl staring at her reflection in a mirror. A joyful family welcoming a soldier home from war. Young faces and old, happy and sad, fresh and careworn. Every once in a while, Charlie froze the picture to point something out. “Look at the life in those eyes.” “See the strength in those hands." And, over and over, "What does that make you feel?"

When the disc was finished, Charlie said, "Okay, tell me—what do you think was so special about his work?"

Michael thought for a moment. "I don't know. His subjects were all so ordinary."

"Bingo!" Charlie said. He grinned at Michael's confusion. "What he did, Michael, was take everyday people doing everyday things and make them memorable.

"You know," he continued as he took the DVD out of the player, "when my daughter gave me this machine, I told her I didn't want it. What would I do with it? I don't rent many movies—most of the ones today aren't worth the money. But then I found I could get other kinds of discs." He tapped the top of the DVD player. "This thing has taken me on tours of cities and museums I never thought I'd see."

He stirred his coffee. "Ever been to an art museum?"

Michael nodded. "There's one in the town Dad's folks live in. And I've seen some shows at the university." He finished the glass of milk. "It must be great to have something you've done hanging where lots of people can see it."

Charlie smiled, and a look came into his eyes that was just like the one Grandpa used to get whenever he was about to tell a story. "When Lucy and I were first married, we went to New York City," he said. "We spent a whole day in the Metropolitan Museum. I felt as if I'd died and gone to heaven—all those wonderful works of art that I'd read about, right there in front of me.

"In one room, there was an empty space on the wall. A painting had been taken down, I don't know why. Lucy said they were just making room for one of my paintings. That became our little joke. Whenever she particularly liked something I'd done, she'd say it was good enough to go in my space at the Metropolitan."

"You never know," Michael said. "Maybe someday . . ."

Charlie shook his head. "I may be good, but not great." He downed the rest of his coffee, then leaned forward and put his hand on Michael's shoulder. "How'd you like that space?"

"Oh, hey," Michael began. But the grip on his shoulder tightened, ever so slightly, and he stopped when he saw the look on Charlie's face. It made him think of Molly when she was afraid nobody believed her.

"All you have to do is want it badly enough," Charlie said. He let go of Michael's shoulder.

The words reminded Michael of another conversation. A conversation at the farm, a couple of years ago.

Do you think I could be an artist, Grandpa?

What? Spend all your time making pictures? Is there a living in that?

I don't know.

But it's what you want to do.

I think so.

Well, Mickey, I don't know much about pictures, so I'm probably not the best person to advise you. All the same, I say go ahead and give it a try. If you want it bad enough, you'll be able to do it, no matter what.

Charlie's voice broke into his thoughts. "It's beginning to cloud up. If you don't want to get caught in the rain, maybe you'd better start for home."

Michael stood up.

"Here, the front door's quicker," Charlie said.

"That's okay," Michael said, heading for the kitchen. "My stuff's in here." He put on his jacket and picked up his backpack. "Anyway, you know what they say—the front door's for company."

"Oh?" Charlie opened the back door. "And what's this one for?"

Michael shot him a grin. "Friends. See you Saturday."

"I don't get it!"

"Shh."

"Sorry." Michael smiled at the school librarian. "It doesn't make any sense," he said to Melanie.

"It does if you think about it," Melanie said. "Look." She pointed at two problems in the book, then copied them onto a piece of paper. "Do you see any difference between these?"

Michael sighed. "One has parentheses?"

"Right." She handed him a pencil. "Now show me how you do them."

Michael took the pencil. He started to write, then stopped. "If the numbers are inside the parentheses, I add them together, then multiply—right?"

"Right."

"So . . . for $2(x + 5)$ equals 42 . . . uh . . ." He began to scribble. "Two into 42 . . . $(x + 5)$ equals 21. And 21 minus 5 is 16. So x equals 16?"

Melanie smiled. "Right. Now the other one."

Michael chewed on the pencil. "$2x + 5$ equals 42. 42

minus 5 equals 37. That means $2x$ is 37. So x equals . . . $18\frac{1}{2}$!"

"See," Melanie said, "I told you you could do it. You're going to do fine on the test tomorrow."

"I hope so."

"And you can keep the pencil," she added with a grin. "I like to chew my own."

Two periods later, when Michael sat down in Mr. Wolf's room, he had a feeling that something wasn't quite right. The Wolfman had a funny little smile on his face. It wasn't long before Michael found out why.

"There's a slight change in routine this week," Mr. Wolf said after the late bell rang. "I know it's only Thursday. But I won't be here tomorrow, so I'm giving you your test today."

Today? Now? Michael glanced over at Melanie.

You can do it, she mouthed.

He wished he could be as sure as she was.

When class was over, Melanie caught up with him in the hall. "Well?" she said.

Michael shook his head. "I don't know," he said. "I think maybe it went all right. But I've thought that before."

They walked along to the cafeteria. Melanie put her backpack on a table and went to get a container of milk.

"Hey, Mike." Brad beckoned from a few tables away.

Michael hesitated, then shook his head. He put his backpack on the table next to Melanie's. By the time he got back with his milk, she was already eating.

"How's your art project going?" she asked.

"Slow. I'm still practicing eyes and noses. I have to get going on it, though. I'm going to enter it in the arts competition."

"Really?"

"Yeah." He took a bite of his sandwich, then continued. "Grandpa might not have been a big kind of hero, but he was mine. He taught me a lot of things, like about fishing and nature and stuff. And we used to just talk a lot."

"He sounds nice."

"He was great. And it's funny. In some ways, Charlie's kind of like him. When he talks to me, it's the same way Grandpa did—like I'm not just a kid. But there's a big difference, too."

"What?"

"Grandpa always used to have these sayings, little bits of advice. He had them for everything, and everyone in the family knew them. Not Charlie, though. At least, not so far."

At dinner that evening, Dad clinked his fork against his water glass. "I have an announcement," he said.

Everyone sat still, waiting.

Dad looked around the table with the beginning of a smile. Then he shook his head. "On second thought, maybe you wouldn't be interested."

"Jim!" Mom looked as if she wanted to grab his ears and shake him.

"Daddy, that's not fair," Jamie said.

Dad's smile grew. "All right," he said. "As you know,

thanks to Mom—who made me go work at the library last Saturday—on Monday I was able to turn the last section of my first draft in to Kirk and my other committee members. Kirk e-mailed me this afternoon that they all read it, and had just a few suggestions. He wants to meet with me on Saturday. After that, I can start writing the final dissertation. So it looks as if there's light at the end of this tunnel at last."

They all clapped and cheered. Mom got up and gave him a big kiss, which made Jamie and Molly giggle.

Michael leaned back and smiled. He hadn't seen Dad this happy in a long time.

After dinner, Michael sat at his desk, studying the photograph of Grandpa.

With one finger, he slowly traced over Grandpa's face. Eyes, nose, jaw. If only he could absorb it all from the paper into his hand.

Picking up a pencil, he began to move it on the blank sheet of paper in front of him.

The lines he drew were so faint that anyone watching would have thought the pencil had no point. He could see them, though. Gradually, they grew darker, and the shapes grew clearer—shoulders, the head, the straw hat he always wore. As the drawing took shape, Michael's pencil strokes shortened, becoming tighter, more controlled. He could almost feel both Grandpa and Charlie there with him, watching, smiling with approval.

When he finally put the pencil down, he looked at his clock.

Nine? He'd been working for two hours? No wonder his hand was stiff.

He stood up and stretched, massaging his hand, then leaned the photo and the sketch pad against the wall and stepped back a bit. He smiled. This was probably the best drawing he'd ever done. Even the shirt, an old plaid flannel one with a missing button, looked good. It was all there but the face itself. He'd wait until tomorrow, when he was fresh, to start that.

He went downstairs to get a glass of milk. Dad was sitting at the kitchen table with a glass of orange juice.

"Hey, sport, come on in," Dad said. "You look beat. Long day?"

"Not really." Michael stretched his neck from side to side. "I've been working on an art project for school. My eyes are tired."

"I know what that's like," Dad said. "So, tell me—how's it been going with Charlie Andrews? You guys getting along?"

"Yeah. I like him. And he's a good teacher. He's let me borrow some books that have really helped with this project."

"Good. I'm going to have to give him a call one of these days. It's been too long. And how's school going?"

Now. Now's the time to ask for help. "Pretty good," Michael said. He took a deep breath. "Except for math."

Dad frowned. "What's up with that?"

"I don't know. I'm trying, but a lot of it just doesn't make sense."

"Who's your teacher?"

"Mr. Wolf."

"Have you talked to him?"

"Once. It didn't do any good. And by now he's made up his mind that I'm a slacker."

Dad thought. "Would it help if I talked with him?"

"Probably not." *Ask him. Go ahead and ask him.*

But Dad beat him to it. "Why haven't you asked me for help?"

Michael fumbled for the right words. "I . . . it's just . . . You have so much going on right now. And I heard you talking with Mom the other morning—you sounded so down about your dissertation. I didn't want to give you anything else to worry about."

"Oh, Michael." Dad rubbed a hand over his face. "Don't ever be afraid to ask me for help with something. I might be busy right when you ask. But I'll do my best to find time. So ask—okay?"

Michael nodded. "Okay. I have a friend helping me, too."

"Great. Together, we'll get you through."

A while later, it felt good to fall into bed and turn out the light. He hadn't felt this tired in a long time. But he hadn't felt this good in a long time, either. He was pretty sure he'd passed the Wolfman's test, the portrait of Grandpa was coming along, and it looked as if they'd be getting Dad back soon. Things were starting to turn around.

Saturday morning, Michael sat at his desk, frowning.

Something wasn't right.

He sighed. Maybe he was too close. He propped the drawing against the wall and stepped back.

It was the eyes. Those weren't Grandpa's eyes.

"Darn it!"

He'd gotten up early to do some work on his art project before he went to Charlie's. Sketches of noses, ears, and eyes covered his desk and the floor around it. He'd been trying to put them all together since yesterday.

Ms. Simmons was right. This wasn't easy. But it was the kind of challenge he liked.

As he gathered up the papers, he looked around the room. It was beginning to look like Charlie's studio, with drawings stuck all over the wall.

He opened his art folder to put the sketches inside. He took out a sketch he'd done of Melanie yesterday. He could still hear Ms. Simmons.

"Michael, this is very good. May I?"

He'd nodded. This was the class where he didn't

mind being singled out. He kept his eyes on his desk while she showed his drawing to the rest of the class, only lifting them to sneak a look at Melanie, who smiled as she listened to Ms. Simmons.

Melanie hadn't said a word about the drawing after class. But Michael smiled now as he remembered that smile. He slipped the drawing back into the folder, then pulled it out again and put it in a large envelope. He'd take it with the others he wanted Charlie to see.

The morning was chilly. His breath made little white puffs as he pedaled. There had been an early frost the other night, enough to start leaves dropping from the trees. They crunched beneath his bike tires. As he turned in at Charlie's driveway, he stopped and looked down the street at Melanie's blue-and-white house. No sign of life. But it was early.

He rode around to the back and went up to the door. He reached out his hand to knock but before his hand hit the wood, the door opened.

"Good morning," a tall, dark-haired woman said. And even though he had never met her before, Michael knew her at once. Her eyes were brown, but they sparkled just like Charlie's.

"You're Jean," he said.

She smiled. "I am," she said, "and you must be Michael. Please come in."

Michael stepped into the kitchen and stood rubbing his cold hands together.

"It's kind of a chilly morning for a bike ride, isn't it?" Jean said. "How about some hot chocolate?"

"Sounds good," Michael said. "Please," he added.

She spooned some fine brown powder into one mug, and a coarser, darker powder into another. As she filled both mugs with steaming water from the kettle on the stove, Michael's nostrils were filled with the aromas of chocolate and coffee. She stirred the hot chocolate for a minute, then put both mugs on a tray. "Dad's in the living room," she said. "Why don't you take this and go on in. Oh, and, Michael," she added as he took the tray, "I want you to know how much I appreciate all the help you've been to him."

"That's okay." Michael tucked his envelope under his arm and took the tray into the living room. Charlie sat in the old flowered armchair with his feet up on the ottoman. Something was missing.

"Where's the Road Runner?" Michael asked as he gave Charlie the coffee.

Charlie took a sip. "I gave him the day off."

They laughed. Charlie's heart didn't seem to be in it, though.

"You met Jean?"

"Uh-huh."

They sat in silence. Michael stirred his hot chocolate, trying not to clink the spoon against the mug.

"What have you got there?" Charlie motioned to the envelope on Michael's lap.

"Some drawings."

"Great. Let's see."

Michael leaned forward and gave him the envelope. Charlie looked through the drawings, taking time to study each one. "This is nice," he said, nodding his head. "Very nice." He frowned. "I've seen her before. Who is she?"

"Her name's Melanie Cook," Michael said. "She lives down the street."

"Cook?" Charlie said. "Cook. Oh—the family that moved into the Wilson place this summer. Of course. I've seen her on her bicycle, or walking her dog. A shaggy mutt with a strange name. Gordon, or George. Something like that."

"Grover," Michael said.

"What?"

"The dog's name is Grover."

"Ah, yes, Grover. Anyway, she seems like a nice girl. The likeness is very good, Michael. When did you do this?"

"This week, in class." He took a sip of hot chocolate. "Charlie, how do you do eyes?"

"Eyes?"

"Yeah. I've been working on my final portrait project. I can get the rest of the face right, but not the eyes."

Charlie chuckled. "Eyes, my boy, are the hardest part of a portrait, probably because eyes are more than two round things in the middle of the face."

"What do you mean?"

"Think about it." Charlie rubbed his hands together. "What do you usually notice first when you look at a face? Eyes. They tell you about a person. Think of all the descriptive phrases—'a beady-eyed villain,' 'wide-eyed innocence.' There was a French writer way back in the 1500s who called eyes the 'windows of the soul.' He really put his finger on it there. Did you know that some people believe that if you reproduce a face, you capture that person's soul?"

"I read that somewhere," Michael said.

"I don't know," Charlie said. "Sometimes I think you have to really care about someone in order to do a good portrait of them, because then you can get beyond the nose and cheekbones to how you truly see that person. You can bring out their soul." He leaned back and lifted one eyebrow. "Does that answer your question?"

"Yeah. I think so."

"Excuse me." Jean stood in the doorway. "Either of you need anything before I go upstairs?"

"We're fine, thanks," Charlie said. "If we do, one of us can get it. We're big boys."

She stuck her tongue out at him and left. Michael stifled a laugh. That was something he'd expect from Jamie, not a grownup. "She's really nice," he said.

"She is," Charlie said. "She just hovers a little too much sometimes." He looked out the window as a gust of wind swirled the leaves in the yard. "Last night, I thought raking those would be a good job for you today. However, the way they're blowing around now, you might have a different opinion. Isn't it funny how sometimes what seems like a good idea to one person doesn't to another?"

Michael opened his mouth, but before he could speak, Charlie said, "Jean thinks I should come back to Chicago with her. I'm not going, though," he added. "This is my home. All my friends are here, all my ties. I don't want to be a burden to her, either. She has her own home and family to take care of."

"It's not as if you're some old geezer who forgets to eat or turn off the stove or something like that," Michael said. "You can take care of yourself."

"That may change, Michael."

"But not for a long time."

"Not necessarily."

The only sound to break the silence was a cardinal whistling outside.

"What's going on, Charlie?" Michael said.

Charlie didn't say anything for a minute. Then he cleared his throat. "Michael, I told you I'd never lie to you. I meant it. I have cancer, Michael. That's why I've been so tired lately, why I haven't been feeling well."

Michael swallowed hard. It was hard to do with a lump the size of an egg in his throat. "Okay. So, what are they going to do?"

"There's not much they can do. I was treated for this a few years ago. Now it's come back, and it's spread. My doctor says it doesn't look good."

Michael concentrated on Charlie's face. Everything else melted away as he tried to digest this. "What does that mean?"

"There's a good chance I'm going to die, Michael. There's no easy way to say it. God knows I wish there were."

Michael stood up. As he looked down at Charlie, his pulse pounded in his head. This couldn't be happening.

"Michael—" Charlie began.

Michael cut him off. "The doctor could be wrong." His voice shook. "They make mistakes. I know they do."

Charlie shook his head.

"It's not true."

"Michael, it is true."

"No!" Michael ran from the room, through the house and out the kitchen door. He gasped as the crisp air slammed into his lungs and burned his wet cheeks. Stumbling down the steps, he grabbed his bike and pedaled as fast as he could down the driveway.

He saw Melanie's bike just before they both went crashing to the pavement.

He wiped his eyes as he got to his feet. He would have helped Melanie up, but she was already rising, holding one knee, her eyes flashing.

"Why don't you watch where you're going?" she sputtered.

"I'm sorry." Michael didn't trust himself to say any more. He kept his eyes on the bicycles lying on the sidewalk.

"Sorry?" She poked his shoulder. "Look at my bike. The fender's bent, and the paint's all scratched. And look at *me*! My jeans are torn, and my knee's bleeding."

"I said I'm sorry." Michael's voice broke.

Melanie cocked her head, trying to see his face. "Michael, what's the matter?"

"Nothing." He squatted down to inspect the damage to his own bike. It didn't look too bad.

"Michael?"

"Nothing. Would you just go away?"

She didn't move. "Don't give me 'nothing.' Something's wrong. Can I help?"

He glared up at her. "Charlie just told me he has cancer and the doctors can't do anything. He's probably going to die. Can you help that?"

Melanie closed her eyes. "Oh, Michael," she said at last, "are you sure?"

"That's what he said."

"That's awful. But at least . . . well, you still have time to spend with him."

"Are you kidding? Why get any closer to him when he's just going to be gone?" Michael turned his attention back to his bike, fussing with a slightly bent spoke. He could feel Melanie's gaze boring into him.

"Does he know you feel this way?" she asked.

"No."

"How's he going to know if you don't tell him?"

He shrugged his shoulders.

"I bet he's scared," Melanie said after a moment.

"Oh, right. He sat there talking about it like he was talking about the weather."

"Michael—" Melanie nudged him with her knee, forcing him to look at her. "You have to talk to him."

"Why?"

"Because he's your friend. Because you care about him."

Michael rose to his feet, clenching and unclenching his fists as he stared into Melanie's stormy eyes. "What do you know about it?" he said as he picked up his bike. "And who asked you?" Without waiting for a reply, he got on his bike and started for home.

Eighteen

His legs must have looked like a blur as he pedaled. And still, he tried to go faster. Right, left, right, left. No, *no*, no, *no*.

When he reached home, he dropped his bike in the yard and raced to the door, fumbling in his pockets for his key. Once he got inside, he locked the door again, as if to keep out what he was running from.

The house was empty. Dad was at the university, and Mom had said she was taking the girls shopping. For once, being alone was scary. Going to the phone, he started to dial T.J.'s number, then stopped. T.J. might not be there, and he didn't need a reminder of how alone he felt right now.

Maybe working would help. He went up to his room and stood the drawing of Grandpa on his desk, against the wall, so he could get a good look at it.

When he was younger, he got so frustrated when he couldn't make something look just the way he wanted it. Grandpa told him not to worry. *I can tell you like what you're doing,* he'd say. *And if you like what you're doing, you'll usually do a good job.*

Well, he was doing a good job on this, except for the eyes. Why couldn't he get them? What he had was good, but not right.

He kept looking at the drawing. As he did, Charlie's words came back to him: *You have to really care about someone in order to do a good portrait.*

Nobody had cared about Grandpa the way he had. He and Grandpa had been special to each other.

Suddenly he leaned forward. He stood up and went closer, then stepped back. It was the same each time. But it couldn't be.

He looked away from the drawing and back again. He covered the lower half of the face with his hand. There was no getting around it.

They were more like Charlie's eyes.

He walked to the window and looked out, watching clouds drift across the sky. Melanie's voice echoed in his ears: *Because you care about him.*

He sat down on his bed and picked up the photo of Grandpa. A tear spattered on the glass. "I like him, Grandpa. I didn't think I would at first, but I do. He's not taking your place. Nobody could. But nobody can take his, either."

He put the photo down and went back to the drawing, studying it carefully. Maybe those eyes weren't so bad. They weren't Grandpa's. But where did it say a hero had to be just one person?

This wasn't helping. He had to find something to take his mind off all this. He went down to the family room, turned on the TV, and began flipping channels. There was the usual Saturday stuff—nature, home repair, fishing.

Suddenly a black-and-white picture appeared. It was a party, and a little man with a big cigar was singing, *"Hello, I must be going . . ."*

Michael listened, stunned. When the song was over, he picked up the remote and turned the TV off. In his head, Charlie's words mingled with Groucho's.

"There's a good chance I'm going to die."

"I cannot stay, I came to say I must be going."

He finally gave in. Tears poured down his face as he cried for Grandpa and for Charlie.

At last, he sat back on the couch, exhausted. He took long, deep breaths, trying to calm his insides. He had almost succeeded when the phone rang, the shrill sound making them start jumping all over again.

It was Dad. "Hi, there," he said. "I didn't expect to find you home. I thought you'd be over at Charlie's."

"I came home early."

"I wanted to ask Mom something. Is she there?"

"No. She and the girls went out."

"Oh, well, it can wait." He paused. "Michael, your voice sounds funny. Is everything all right?"

Michael couldn't keep his voice from shaking. "Not really."

"What's up?"

"It's Charlie. He's really sick. He just told me. He said he might die."

"Oh, God." For a moment, Dad didn't say anything else. Then, he said, "Michael, listen—do you want me to come home?"

"What?"

"Do you want me to come home? I can be out of here as soon as I explain to Kirk."

"What about your meeting?"

"I'll reschedule it. Don't you worry about that."

Michael's head reeled. Dad would do this? "But, Dad, you've been working for this—"

Dad cut him off. "Michael," he said in a gentle voice, "I know it hasn't seemed like it much lately, but you are important to me. More important than this meeting. If you want me to come home now, I'll come."

Michael squeezed his eyes shut to stop the tears that threatened to start again. "That's okay, Dad. Do your meeting."

"You sure?"

"Yeah."

"All right. We're supposed to start in a few minutes. I don't know how long it'll last. Maybe an hour, or a little more. I'll leave the minute we're done. You sit tight, and I'll be home as soon as I can."

Michael hung up the phone. "Thank you," he whispered. He picked his jacket up from the floor where he'd dropped it. He'd be here when Dad got home. But before that, there was something he had to do.

The wind had died down and the sun had come out,

warming the day. Michael pedaled slowly at first, gradually picking up speed. As he turned onto Maple Street, he saw Melanie walking Grover. It looked as if she'd turned her torn jeans into cutoffs.

He approached her cautiously, half expecting her to turn and walk away. But she stood there waiting for him.

"Hi, Michael."

"Hi." He glanced at the large bandage on her right knee. "You okay?"

She nodded. "It hurts, but I'll be all right. How about you?"

"Same."

She gave him a little smile. "Good." She hesitated, then said, "Are you going back to Charlie's?"

"Yeah." He spun a pedal with his toe. "Listen, I'm really sorry about your bike."

"You didn't do it on purpose."

"I know. I was thinking that maybe I could touch up the scratches. I've done it before, on my bike."

"Okay. My dad's going to the hardware store later, I think. I can ask him to get the paint."

"Great. It shouldn't take a lot. Tell him I'll pay for it."

"All right. See you later."

Michael rode on down the street. When he reached Charlie's house, he leaned his bike against the back steps and went up to the door. He knocked quietly, then louder.

Charlie answered the door. They looked at each other through the screen.

Michael swallowed, took a deep breath, and said in a steady voice, "I heard you need some leaves raked."

Charlie smiled. "Interested in the job?"

"Maybe."

Charlie's smile broadened. He opened the door. "Come on in," he said. "Let's talk about it."

Michael stepped inside. "Okay," he said. "Let's talk."